P.I.

Murder in Olongapo City

P.I. 75:

Murder in Olongapo City

Author R. T. Williams

DISCLAIMER

This is a work of fiction. Names, characters, businesses, places, events, locales, and incidents are either the products of the author's imagination or used in a fictitious manner. Any resemblance to actual persons, living or dead, or actual events is purely coincidental. The opinions expressed are those of the characters and should not be confused with the Author's.

P.I. 75:
Murder in Olongapo City

Cover design: Cyndie Widmer

Publisher:

www.enidbookscorp.com
enidbookscorp@yahoo.com

DEDICATION

Dedicated to Robert L Williams 1919-1985
(Dad)

PROLOGUE

1975
Subic Bay, U.S. Naval Base
Olongapo City, Philippines

"Ricky, you come right now to Shit River. Denny B say, 'Ricky Ticky Jackson.'"

I'm shaken out of my reverie by a twelve-year-old street boy who everybody calls Jackson. I down my Jack, tell Joe and Lettie I'll be back, then split.

New Year's Eve in Olongapo City. It's only 1500 hours and shit's already hitting the fan. The USS Midway is in port along with its battle group; more sailors about to be drunk, fucked-up, and laid than you can count, and even more hookers than that. Jackson and I double-time it back down the main drag toward the naval base, then take a left on Gordon Street, go through some small alleys, and take a right down to the floating cesspool that's in that part of Olongapo, the river known to sailors worldwide as "Shit River." When we get there Denny is smoking a Lucky Strike and talking to one of the River Queens, good looking girls who stand in small Bonka Boats and beg pesos

1

from the GIs as they cross the river over a bridge. The girl Denny is talking to is crying, and Denny's consoling her, taking some notes, and palming her ass.

"Ricky-san, didn't mean to fuck up your holiday, but Miss River Boat here turned up a US corpse," Denny says, pointing behind him.

"She so fat and ugly, she stink booku," the girl says between sobs.

Behind Denny, some MPs and corpsmen are pulling the bloated, stinking corpse of a black man out of the river. The stench is overwhelming. His clothes have burst at the seams because of his swollen body, now they're just rags. This corpse being black means it's most likely a GI, which means some work for Denny and me. Denny B is my partner at MIS, the Military Investigative Service. We are stationed on the Subic Bay Naval Base, in the Philippine Islands (P.I.)- Olongapo City is part of the area we're assigned to cover. This case is most likely just routine paperwork for a drug overdose; bag him and tag him and send the body back to the world. The medical examiners are on Christmas leave so the body was put on ice in the Naval Regional Medical Center at Cubi Point. When they return, they'll open it up to determine cause of death. As of now, the corpse is a John Doe. Since there's nothing much we can do right now, I head back over to Papa Joe's for a drink, and Denny goes to file a preliminary report at headquarters - HQ.

CHAPTER 1

The ice cubes made a slight cracking sound as the smooth brown liquid hit them. Jack on the rocks is mellow anywhere, but here at the Green Dolphin Lounge, listening to *Lee Morgan* blow and Papa Joe Pettaway preach—it's damn near nirvana. Papa Joe's going on about the Ali-Frazier fight, the "Thrilla in Manila" we'd seen live at Araneta a short time back.

"Juney, them's the baddest heavyweights I ever seen. Louis, Charles, Marciano—they never fought challengers of their own caliber in their prime. But these dudes, man, fire and ice."

Dragging on a Kool, I nod my head, sip my Jack and think, Papa Joe's seen it all: sixty or more years old from South Kakalaki, a Montford Point Marine, Silver Star from Iwo Jima, Top Sarge, a World War II and Korea Vet, and a bar owner and Papasan here in Olongapo, with many wives and kids. What a life.

"Ali so Pogi, I glad he win. Frazier a monkey," says Lettie, a young hooker from Cebu City.

At this, Papa Joe raises an eyebrow, and I know the sermon's about to start. "That's why the ofays[1] rule the world. That bull jive like Little

---

[1] Ofays - Slang derogatory word for white folks

Bit over there is spoutin', two bad blacks – Princes - beating each other down for the ofays' profit and enjoyment, and Ali plays right into this shit with all that gorilla this-and-that. Man, back in the forties and fifties, these dames over here and in Japan used to look at our asses to make sure we didn't have tails because the damn crackers told them we were goddamn apes. Can you dig that, man? Us brothers got to wake up."

"Go on, Pops," I say, as I've heard many variations on this theme in the ten-plus years I've known him. I met Papa Joe right here in this bar in 1964. I was a nineteen-year-old mess cook on my first P.I. Liberty, and my first night in Olongapo City—the two-square-mile den of iniquity that had sprung up outside the huge US Naval Facility at Subic Bay and served as the 7th Fleets' R&R playground. As I walked down the dusty main drag, Magsaysay Boulevard, in my trop white longs I was blown away by the heat and humidity. It had me sweating right through my skivvies. The smell of raw sewage combined with barbecue chicken, monkey, dog, and whatever else was grilling - man, it was sensory overload.

Jeepneys[2] painted up like psychedelic posters; tricycles, streets packed with men, kids, and more good-looking little hammers than I'd ever seen in one place. Everything was for sale - clothes, shoes, jewelry, food, booze, and much pussy. Every club had a barker at the door and the latest music blasting inside; *The Beatles, Dave Clark Five, Four Seasons, Gerry and the Pacemakers*—cool for white boys, but nothing for the brothers to groove on. Little-kid pickpockets were begging and stealing at the same time. A kid begging for money said, "Brothers, go to Rizal Street," and pointed to the end of the drag. I gave him a peso, and he led me to the spot.

Looking to my left, I saw clubs with names like Birdland, Freeman Club, and Smalls Far East. I was hearing *Little Anthony and the Imperials, Martha Reeves, and James Brown,* felt like back home on Western and Twenty-Ninth in LA, or wherever a brother was from in the world. Man, this was heaven. The chicks were fly Asian soul sisters in tight skirts and spiked heels, with big pretty legs and long black hair. As I walked toward all this Far East soul, I

---

[2] Jeepneys - Tricked-out, brightly painted Jeep Willys that are common throughout P.I.

heard the clear, hard bop sound of the cooker - *Lee Morgan*'s hit "*The Sidewinder*" was blaring from down a small alley. I looked up and saw a wood carving of a dolphin painted green with the words "Green Dolphin Bar and Lounge," hanging over a door. I walked inside, it was cool and dark. Some older brothers were sitting around, talking trash with the bartender, a short muscular dude with close-cropped salt-and-pepper hair, a neatly trimmed gray beard, and a gold front tooth.

"What you want, Junior Flip? This here's a Vets' bar. Go on down the street with them other jitterbugs." These were Papa Joe's first words to me.

"Man, when I hear *Morgan* blow, I got to check it out. *Lee's* my main man," I said.

"Well, all right, Joe. This youngblood is hip. Give him a taste," RL Rossell said, laughing. RL was Joe's homeboy and friend from South Kak.

"Okay, Junior Flip, what you drinkin'?" Joe asked.

"I'll take one of those San Miguel's," I said.

"Bullshit! You drink like a man in here. White or dark, baby?" Joe snarled.

"Gimme what he's drinking," I said, pointing at

RL's drink. It was my first Jack on the rocks. We listened to more sounds: *Basie, Eckstine, Miles, Bird*—even some *'Trane.* I had a few more tastes and was starting to feel no pain. I was standing at the bar when Papa Joe braced me and threw a quick left hook at my head, but I saw it comin' and blocked it. What I didn't see or hear was the butterfly knife in his right hand, which was at my throat.

"An attack never comes where you can see it, Juney," Joe said. That was my new nickname, Juney, short for Junior Flip. After that night, Joe became like a father to me. Anytime I was in P.I., it was always Papa Joe's where I hung out.

I down the rest of my Jack and leave Papa Joe's so I could spend the remainder of New Year's Eve with my main lady and steady girlfriend, Nea Santos. I'd brought her onto the base for a good meal and some drinks. Then we rang in the New Year properly in my quarters on base, the Cubi Point Bachelor Officers' Quarters— the BOQ. Nice, clean, quiet, with a maid, and houseboy—a good place to unwind and think.

I'd met Nea in 1972 while serving on the Ranger. We spent some great R&R time together back then. When I was assigned as a civilian to Subic with MIS a couple of years later, we ran into each other and picked up where we left off. Nea and I maintained a small hooch just outside the base in Barrio Barretto. It was clean and neat, thanks to Nea. I called her Blue because she always wore an outfit in some shade of blue when she was working. Even at age twenty-two, when I met her, she was already a Mamasan[3] with three to five girls in her stable from her home of San Fernando. She has the classic Coca-Cola body: 34-24-35, more tail than most Filipinas, about whom GIs often said had a case of "noassatol"—no ass at all. As for Nea, she never sold her ass like a carnival ride. She found a GI and stuck with him. Although I was a civilian, she stuck with me now.

I know Nea to be mestiza[4], which I figure accounts for her build. She is five feet three inches of stone fox—a knockout. I, on the other hand, am five feet eleven, two hundred pounds and consider myself African American. My mom was from the Dominican Republic, and my pop was a redbone from Charleston, South Carolina which accounts for my light-

[3] Papasan/Mamasan– a man/woman who manages female workers in bars and brothels.
[4] Mestiza - A woman of mixed race

brown complexion and thick, straight hair. My facial features are somewhat long and thin, leading most people to wonder about my racial or ethnic background. My one distinguishing feature is a long scar running from the bridge of my nose to the middle of my right cheek. I often wear some Ray-Ban shades to draw attention away from it.

"Ricky, you a good-looking guy. I think that scar is pogi[5]," Nea remarks, while lightly running her index finger over it as we sit together in the big Papasan chair in my room.

"Right, baby girl. That's what all you fine hammers tell me," I reply.

"Ricky, how did you really get that scar?" Nea presses.

"I told you, some Cholos cut me trying to get me to give up my boys when I rolled with the Businessmen back in LA," I say, chuckling.

"That's some bullshit, Ricky."

"Okay, doll, I'll tell you the real deal 'cause until we started going with each other, you never asked and never stared." This scar is usually the first thing anyone that gets to know me for

---

[5] Pogi - Handsome

a while asks about. "Truth is, a dude from Hamilton High cleated me in a football game, just missed my eye. Never found out which cat it was, but he marked me for life," I say.

"Rick, I still think you guapo, scar and all," Nea says, kissing the scar up and down my face.

"Well, doll, in two days they gonna open up that brother we found floating, and Denny B and me might have some action," I remark.

"No way, Rick, just another dopehead lost in Olongapo City," Nea says matter-of-factly.

CHAPTER 2

January 2, 1976, my thirty-first birthday. Denny and I are assigned as the leads for investigating the New Year's Eve floater. I go over to the medical examiner's room to see what they find. The room is refrigerator-cold and has a wall of antiseptic stainless-steel lockers on one side. The square locker door marked number twelve is opened, and the bloated body of the young man who washed up in Shit River is slid out on a metal slab. One arm falls slightly as the body is being lifted from the meat locker to the examination table, a finger catches on the table's edge and pops off, falling to the deck.

"Man, this kid is ripe. Hey, photog, give us a hand here with the stiff," Doc Lefkowitz, Navy Commander and Forensic Specialist, says to the young navy photographer. As Doc conducts the autopsy, the photog will document it on film for further study. The face is badly decomposed, and the body is like a large greenish-brown balloon. The core section is grotesquely bloated, but the extremities and genitals remain of normal proportion. Doc starts with an external examination and points out that the fingers have been mutilated, rendering them unprintable. Doc instructs the photographer to shoot various angles of the body. I can't tell if this is the regular photo guy or not because of the gear he has on, but he has the same twin-lens Mamiya Camera they always use—it gives a larger negative for more detail in the blowups. Because of the swollen condition of the corpse, Doc opens him up first, then examines the flip side. But the cause of death is evident with just an external look-see. The body has very long hair, which isn't unusual for brothers in the Navy. They grease their hair, wear two or three nylon stocking caps at night, get a shape-up around the ears and neck, and wear a cover while on duty. But once out on the beach, they pick that bad boy out and its hello Sly Stone. "Well, this is what did this fellow in," Doc says, pointing to a small hole at the base of the skull that had been obscured by all that hair. The shot is right behind the left ear. As I look and the photo guy snaps, I think it looks like a pro hit with a .22. This is very strange for P.I.

"Ricky, you don't need to stay. You can pick up the prints at the photo lab in the afternoon," Doc says.

As I'm leaving, I hear the high-pitched sound of

the small circular saw, and Doc saying, "Okay, let's take his lid off," The eerie sound continues as the saw cuts through the skull. I get out of my coveralls, which have the stench of rotted refuse embedded in them. The funk remains in my nose and on my body. I need to hit the rain room for a shower, but I have to update Denny first. I dial MIS from Doc's office and ask for Denny. He picks up and I say, "Hey, buddyro, bad news. Our floater was offed, and it looks like a pro job."

"Hold on, shipmate, there ain't no pro jobs in P.I., just blow jobs. Wait till we get the flicks before you jump to conclusions," Denny says between sips of joe and drags on a Lucky.

"Well, we can check that out at the photo lab later today. I'm going to hit the BOQ and wash some of this funk off. I'll see you at the lab at 1600 hours," I say.

"Roger, Mac Dodger," Denny replies.

By the time Denny and I hooked up at the photo lab, Doc Lefkowitz had called MIS HQ to relay that a prophylactic filled with white powder was found inside the anus of the corpse. The powder was sent out to be analyzed. The photo lab was a good-size one-story building with three darkrooms and a small berthing area for the duty crew. It was run by a mealy-mouthed Warrant Officer and two pompous chief petty officers—CPOs—one of whom made his racist views on spades, spics, and slopes known to all who came in his wake. senior chief photographer's mate, DeForest. He was part of the white "good ol' boy" fleet of the recent past. Admiral Zumwalt had done much to bring the Navy into the 1970's by offering access to better rates and promotion opportunities to minority sailors so DeForest was becoming a relic in his beloved US Navy. Because of his bigoted ways, Denny and I liked to yank his chain. As civilian GS-12's, we outranked him, and as MIS Agents could put him in a real hurt locker. That's why we went right in, past the third-class personnel man at the front desk, directly back to Manny's color darkroom. Manny was the master color printer who did all the autopsy blowups. He was a real craftsman, a mid-thirties Filipino who was a naturalized US citizen.

"Kamusta ka na, Manny[6]?" Denny bellowed.

"Fuck off, Denny B. I just got the negs a couple hours ago," Manny replied with a grin. We both

---

[6] Kamusta ka na – What's up?

knew he probably had triplicates of the pertinent views done in eight by ten already. At this point, DeForest walks into the room and starts talking smack to me and Denny.

"Well, if it isn't Frick and Frack, the government's solution to integration. Just walk right in to my photo lab without checking in. I must say I feel honored. What's the occasion?"

"Just here to check out Manny's handiwork," I say.

"You know, for a bottle washer, he does an adequate job. In a few years, with all Zummie's new regs in place, this job will be all affirmative action. Gomez and these coloreds and greasers from CONUS[7] that are volunteering—they're the bottom of the barrel, but we're equal opportunity now," Deforest says, smirking and looking me dead in the eye.

"Yeah, equal opportunity started back in the fifties when they let needle-dick, wet brains like you into the fleet. Ricky and I got work to do, so shove off fat boy," Denny says. The laughter was barely contained in the lab by all within earshot of Denny's salvo. Deforest turned beet red and went back to his office, vowing to

---

[7] CONUS – Continental United States

report Denny. When Deforest slammed his office door, everyone in the room cracked up laughing. Manny gave Denny five, and Denny says, "I just saved that dumb shit's life, and he don't even know it. But if he kept smirking at Ricky like that much longer, it was gonna be lights-out."

We all chuckled a little more. But Denny was right. Despite being a cop, I still had a quick and violent temper once it was set off, and it was usually the smirk or silly grin from shit-for-brains like Deforest that could light my fire.

Manny showed us the prints, which were of outstanding quality—very sharp and in vivid color. There's also shots of some small bullet fragments and the prophylactic of powder. They couldn't recover enough fragments to get any type of ballistics on the bullet. The head was decomposed beyond recognition, and the body showed no birthmarks or tattoos, just a few scratches that probably happened postmortem, and of course no fingerprints. I asked who the photog was that took the flicks? Manny answered, "A new kid, Smitty, took 'em. Johnny Smith, he's a black kid from DC or Philly, that Deforest can't stand, but he's a good photographer and lab tech."

"Is Smitty still around? I'd like to talk to him," I say.

"No, that guy leaves right at 1600, got a hooch out in the barrio with a local girl," Manny says.

"Local girl, not a hooker?" Denny asks.

"No, a seamstress from the barrio," Manny sighs.

"Hey, KC still out in that trailer?" I ask, referring to CPO Streeter, my old buddy from the Coral Sea.

"Yeah, he's out back working on that bike of his," Manny replies.

Denny took the prints and went back to the cop shop. I went around back to find my old shipmate, who was indeed working on his vintage Indian motorcycle. KC was pushing forty, a big bear of a guy with reddish hair and a full beard, tattoos up and down both arms, steel-gray eyes, and a flattop haircut.

"Qué pasa, Capone?" KC says in a cool Chicano manner. "Capone" is my old nickname from LA, I got it because of the scar. KC was from Fresno, he was the only white boy to ride with the Latin Pagans in the fifties. He enlisted in '56 or '57, and he's one of the few dudes in the Navy who can call me Capone to my face.

"Same-o, same-o, man. Another floater, Manny's doing the prints. This one's getting weird. Found some kind of powder, probably horse, on the body. It looks like he was knocked off by a pro," I say. "What's up with that kid Smitty who took the flicks?" I ask as KC sits down on a stool near his bike, reaches into a cooler, and grabs a couple San Migs for us—cold and frosty in the P.I. heat.

"Well, that kid's been here about a year, but Deforest has him cleaning the heads and painting the buildings, all the shit gigs. If a shitty photo shoot like an autopsy comes up, he draws it. He's a trained photog with a good eye, just the wrong color scheme," KC says.

"Yeah, I can dig that. Deforest needs an attitude adjustment." I say.

"Hey, Cap, I hear Rolfie's got a joint up in Manila now." Rolf "Rolfie" Rommag is a German national who's married to a Japanese woman. Together they own a couple of nightclubs in Japan, one in Yokosuka that caters to US sailors and marines, and one in Yokohama whose clientele is mostly European and American businessmen. But the club in Manila is primarily designed for Japanese executives who are starting to frequent Southeast Asia for

19

sex vacations. Japan is becoming an economic superpower, and its citizens have lots of disposable cash for the first time since 1945 when they surrendered to the US. Old Rolfie intends to get as much of that cold hard cash as he can.

"Yeah man, he calls the joint Daktari. He has a gross of hookers from all over the far East. Man, It's freak city. We got to make a run up there soon." I say.

"Yeah, I'm looking to trade Mimi and Fifi in for some newer models." Mimi and Fifi are KC's live-in maids, who treat him like a sultan and walk around his place in nothing but flip-flops and bikini bottoms at all times.

"Well, that's on you, dude. We could use the R&R."

"It's I&I for me—intoxication and intercourse," KC says as we slap five and promise to hook up on a Manila run.

I head back to the HQ to see if anything has developed with our John Doe floater. His autopsy picture had been disseminated among all the CO's on the bases at Subic and Cubi Point, and to the ships currently in port. The face was so badly decomposed that the autopsy photos would probably not yield a definitive ID. Doc Lefkowitz said he'd probably been dead three or four days when he washed up which meant there were several other ships that needed to be contacted. Because of transfers, leaves, temporary assigned duty -TAD- orders and so on, it could be quite a while before we could ID the body. The prophylactic, however, contained about fourteen grams of 95 percent pure China-white heroin.

CHAPTER 3

I headed off base on foot, across the Shit River Bridge towards the main drag, Magsaysay Boulevard. Magsaysay is still a trip on the senses; hot, humid air mixed with the smells of gasoline, food grilling on open flames, garbage, and a myriad of street sounds. It's similar to 1964, but the people and clubs were different. No more *Beatles* and *Dave Clark Five*. Now the main drag was disco and heavy metal. The Jug Jug Club was blasting *"Fly, Robin, Fly"* from a huge outdoor speaker. The Old Club Mexicali was now the Foxy Brown, and *Van McCoy's "Hustle"* was its new theme song. The crowd looked different, too. No more trop white longs or tropical khakis, it was civvies now; platform shoes, polyester bell-bottoms, silk shirts, and afros on many brothers. Jeans and T-shirts were the common uniform, and hookers were in all states of dress and undress. As I passed the High Plains Club, the loud rock music of the house band was winding up a crowd with a perfect rendition of *"Free Bird."* At the corner of Magsaysay and Rizal Street was the club 7th Heaven, the first and only club on the main drag that catered to Black GIs. A group of Marines were in front of the 7th exchanging long, intricate handshakes and fist bumps known as daps, which were ways brothers had developed to greet one another in Korea and then in Nam. The short-time dap told your brother that you were not over him or he over you, and you would have each other's backs. Much more could be added to tell what unit you were with and where you had fought. It could take a group of marines several minutes to dap properly.

I crossed Rizal and walked down the alley to Papa Joe's. It was around 2000 hours. On entering Joe's, I noted that there was a smattering of older GIs and a few veteran hookers. Joe and Baby Sis were behind the bar, Sis making drinks and Joe DJ'ing. He had *Coleman Hawkins's "The Hawk Flies High"* on the system.

"Juney, where you been at, boy? That stiff got your nose to the grindstone?" Joe asks, laughing.

"Sis, let me get a Jack on ice," I say, lighting a Kool. "Pops, there is some deep kimchi[8] with this one. Looks like it wasn't no accident or OD."

---

[8] Kimichi – Deep shit (Korean cabbage that smells bad)

Joe looks at me out of the corner of his eye and says, "You know them Frogs was running around this camp awhile back? They show up and shit follows."

The Frogs were Derrick "Deke" and Ty "Deadeye", two Black Underwater Demolition Team Seals who made their peace with God and man in Nam, Cambodia, and Laos. Now it was said that they were mercenaries. They worked in Africa, South America, the Middle East, or wherever they could blend in with the indigenous population and snatch, rip off, or bump off a target.

"Yeah, Pops, but they don't leave bodies floating. Maybe chopped up like hamburger and growing rice, but not with two arms, two legs, and a head."

"What I'm saying Juney, is them fellas was here, and you got a stiff on your doorstep. Dead mickey fickeys is their calling card," Joe replies, making an excellent point. I sip my Jack, and Joe tells me about seeing the *Hawk* in '36 with *Fletcher Henderson* in Harlem. The *Hawk* was his clarion call to Jazz, just as twenty-five years later, *Lee Morgan* was mine. Despite our age difference, we were Jazz brothers to the heart. During the time we'd known each other, Papa Joe and I had often discussed his reasons for leaving the US for good. Joe told me how, while stationed in DC in the mid-fifties, he hadn't been allowed to try on a pair of shoes at a downtown department store. He was in his early forties at the time, a World War II and Korea Vet, still on active duty; a Gunnery Sergeant, Silver and Bronze Stars, and two Purple Hearts, but a black man in full dress uniform still couldn't try on a pair of shoes in the nation's capital, or for that matter, get a sandwich or a cup of coffee. Not just in D.C., but throughout the South and in many Northern Cities as well. Joe said he could risk his life and take the lives of others in the name of American Democracy, in every corner of the world, but there was no Democracy for a black man in his homeland, that same America. Joe said to me, "If I got to be treated like I'm not a citizen, then I'll live where I'm not one," This made a lot of sense to me. I, too, had seen the hypocrisy of the land of the free—the two-tier racial caste system, the ridiculous wealth and dire poverty. But as much as I despised those things, America, with its big fast cars, big fine women, and sweet soul music, was, I believed in my heart, still the place where you could dream big and grab the brass ring. I would never leave for good, as Papa Joe had.

"Hey, Joe, put some organ grinders on," I say. Joe plays *"The Sermon" by Jimmy Smith*, with my man *Morgan* on horn. I sip my Jack and mull over the new case in my head. I couldn't stop thinking about the John Doe floater and his mutilated fingers. Somebody sure didn't want him to be ID'd. His death was no crime of passion; it was straight-up murder one. I needed to talk to Doc Lefkowitz and that kid, Smitty to see if they noticed anything the photos might not have shown. I finish my third Jack at around 2230, say my good-byes to Joe and the crew and head to catch a Jeepney to Nea's and my crib in Barrio Barretto.

It was a Friday night, I always try to be out of Olongapo before 2330 because at that time, PO Town pitches a bitch. The bars close, and the drunk, high and horny denizens have till midnight to clear the streets. The hookups, dope deals, and other transactions are happening at a fevered pitch. The sailors and marines all want one of them LBFM's, the universal GI acronym for the P.I. bar girls; Little Brown Fucking Machines. I would be home before the nightly melee got under way. There's a curfew of midnight for all US Military personnel and Philippine civilians imposed by the US backed strongman, Ferdinand Marcos, and enforced by his notorious Police Constabulary, a/k/a, "PC." But at 2200 hours, it's jumping at the High Plains Club. Their number one band and Enrique Paz, their guitar ace, are laying down *Deep Purple's "Smoke on the Water"* to absolute perfection. The bikini-clad go-go girls are shaking and gyrating, their brown bodies glistening with sweat. The High Plains is the top club, with the best Rock Band in P.I. They cater to the young white Sailors and Marines who consider themselves heads; many spending whole paychecks on drinks for the ladies, dancers, and hostess while swigging San Miguel, Mojo, Shake-em up, or whatever concoction they can dream up. Down the street at the Foxy Brown a mixed crowed of black, white, and Latin GIs are diggin' the disco sound of their house band playing the hit of the moment, *"Love Won't Let Me Wait."* Out on the floor, the couples are grinding hard. A large black marine is whispering in the ear of his beautiful, petite dance partner that he can't wait and needs her now. She tells him to wait till closing at 2330 so he can save paying the Mamasan her bar fine and give her the extra ducats. *"Love's got me high . . ,"* the singer croons.

On Gordon Street the white lifers and rednecks are in their shit-kicking cowboy bars. At Club Viking, a hulking, buzz-cut marine is telling his Filipino girlfriend that if he even hears that she's looking at or talking to any niggers, he'll cut her face up, and if any spades come into Club Viking, he'll burn it down with her and the rest of the slopes in it. At the far end of Gordon Street, a tall, trim, bald officer is telling Conception Ramos, the club owner and Mamasan, that the last girl she'd sent him was too old and developed. Ramos protests that she was only thirteen, and that she told her his genitals were large and hurt her. The bald man gives Ramos a hundred US dollars and tells her there's four hundred more for a real young cherry girl. At the corner of Magsaysay and Rizal in the 7th Heaven, the DJ is jamming the O'Jays song "For the Love of Money," and a Benny boy, a transvestite, known as Starchild, is nervously sipping a lady's drink. He knows he should not be in there in drag. The 7th is a club for straight Black and Latin GIs, and they can get very violent when their China Doll turns out to be a China Boy. But that night, Starchild is one of the baddest-looking hammers in the 7th.

The Jeepney I boarded on Rizal Street had only two other passengers; a Black Sailor and a small, thin Asian-looking hooker with an Afro. Asian soul sisters were in every US base town from Pearl Harbor to U-Tapao - facsimiles of the real African American sisters back in the world, but with their own Asian sensibility. For me, they were like Japanese Suntory Whiskey. It could get you bent but was nowhere near the real Kentucky thing. I preferred the Asian women I dealt with to be themselves, proud of their own background and heritage. That was the way Nea was, even when working for the enjoyment of U.S. GI's, Nea and her crew retained their distinctive long hair and almost makeup-free faces. They did, however, wear the jeans, halter tops, and platform shoes that were popular stateside.

The couple got off the Jeepney at the Victory Liner Station at the edge of the City, where an old fellow was hawking, "Balut! Balut!" Balut was the almost fully formed duck still in its egg that was eaten by men as an aphrodisiac. A few more folks, mostly vendors and tailors and such, got on board the Barrio-bound Jeepney. It was 2245, still a little early for the masses of

Sailors and hookers, but the rush would start soon. The Jeepney crossed the Shit River upstream from the Subic footbridge, at this point the River was rotten, filthy, and stench-ridden; but way upstream, deep in the jungle, this river was pristine enough to swim and fish in. Once it passed through the Naval Base and Olongapo City it became a biohazard. Our hooch overlooked Subic Bay and had a beautiful view of Grande Island and the port. It was three rooms and a wash area. We had running water and enough electricity for my stereo, some fans, lights, and Nea's sewing machine. It was a Singer electric that I got her from the Base Exchange—the BX—to replace her foot-pedal model. Nea was an outstanding seamstress and made clothes for herself and a few other women. The old couple we rented from loved Nea and accepted me. They watched out for our place, and the fact that I was a MIS cop kept the local rip-off boys away.

I got a beer and put *Four & More* by *Miles* on my system. *Tony Williams* and *George Coleman* straight up smoke on that set. By midnight, Nea hadn't shown, so I figured she was with one of her steady customers, a married navy commander who managed to get away from his wife on duty nights. The relationship Nea and I had was loose, but respectful. She still had a couple of high-paying customers, and I hung loose on occasion myself. We never brought anyone else to our crib and were always careful about using protection with others. Weird? Maybe, but that was monogamous for P.I.

Nea and I sometimes spoke of America, or "the world," as the GIs called it. Unlike most bar girls, she had spent time in the States on a fiancée visa, the dude she was with was a black air force sergeant and she got a taste of American Racism 101. She was shunned by other Filipinos or Filipinas who were married to whites and regarded with contempt and suspicion by both black and white women. She also saw the American Caste System, in which blacks were at the bottom of the barrel. She's always quoting this rhyme a kid told her in San Bernardino, California, where she was living - "If you white, you all right; if you yellow, you mellow; if you brown, stick around; but if you black, get way back." That pretty much summed up America for Nea. She would never live there. She returned to P.I. in 1971 and set out to be an independent woman. At age twenty-five she had her own club, seamstress business, and several girls working for her. She was well on her way. She had built a nice house in her hometown near San Fernando. She said I could live with her there when we retired, but she would not come stateside with me. I knew that, flaws and all, I'd return to Southern California where I was born and bred.

I flipped the LP to the B-side and began to reflect how football had charted the course of my life. The scar on my face was always the first thing people noticed about me, which is why I usually wear sunglasses. Football gave me direction, determination, and a channel for my anger. My brother, Reynaldo, was six years older than I was and had starred as a split end at Jefferson in the mid-1950s. I made varsity as a sophomore at Manual Arts in 1960. I played wingback, safety, and return man. I ran a ten-flat hundred yards, pads didn't slow me up much. I had outstanding football speed, along with aggression, anger, and a passion for the game. I loved to hit receivers and running backs. I was 185 pounds, could bring most running backs down by myself, and flat wipe out most skinny, fast receivers. They wouldn't run their routes my way more than a couple of times. In my junior and senior years, Manual won the LA City Championships. I had my best game in my senior season of 1962. I ran a kickoff and an interception in for touchdowns and forced a fumble, all against my nemesis, Hamilton High. After that game, some clean brothers in sharkskin Italian suits and processed hair gave me an envelope and said, "Youngblood, you took care of business, and we're businessmen. You keep messing these chucks up on the field and you got a pass from here to Watts." There was two hundred dollars in the envelope. I made it to Long Beach State on a football scholarship but blew my knee out in Summer ball. College wasn't my thing, so I quit and went into the US Navy in December of 1963, right after President Kennedy was popped. I've been roaming the world with the Navy ever since.

Nea got in at 6 a.m., right before I left for base, she was accompanied by her Uncle Ernie, a Police Constabulary. She told me a GI got rough with one of her girls just after curfew, so she got Ernie to tighten him up and turn him over to the AFP[9]. Ernie and I crossed paths professionally from time to time, he was also a

---

[9] AFP – Armed Forces Police

good friend of Papa Joe's.

"Thanks for looking out for my honey-co, Uncle E," I say.

"Family first, Ricardo," Ernie replies with a wink. He kisses Nea's cheek, waves good-bye, gets back in his Toyota and drives off toward Subic City.

"Look, doll, I'm headed to base. This case could be real heavy. I might be crashing at the BOQ for a while,"

"Ricky, I understand your work, but right now I'm crashing right here," Nea says. I kiss her and split for the base as she hits the rag pile for some shut-eye.

At HQ, Jerry Tyler, the lead agent of our Division of Criminal Investigations, calls roll and reviews our assignments. At this early stage, it's pretty much an all-hands effort—all eleven agents and Tyler gathering any intel we can. Tyler motions Denny and me into his office.

"Gents, we still have no positive ID on our John Doe floater, but we have some leads pointing to a First-Class Aviation Electrician named Phillip Goins. He was TAD from the Ranger, assisting in training folks on the EA6B[10] Aircraft. He was supposed to have reported in at the Naval Air Station in Memphis on December 29, but never showed. Goins is black and in his early thirties. We're checking his dentals now," Tyler states in his nasal twang.

"So, what was his major malfunction? Doper, skivvy hound, fag, or just a fuck-up in general?" Denny asks.

"Well, Denny, that's the rub," Tyler says. "Seems Goins was a squared-away sailor and family man. Such an outstanding tech that the tech reps from Grumman Corporation that make the EA6B, requested him to assist them with this training."

"WTF, Skip, did his old lady Jody his ass? AJ—squared or not, home slice had a bag of pure China boy up his turd cutter, and a small-caliber round in his dome, and that shit don't add up, even in PO Town," I say.

"Point taken, Rick. That's why I want you and Denny out front on this one. Olongapo is the number one R&R spot for the 7th Fleet. Music, booze, hookers, maybe a little grass, but we keep the hard stuff out. There's been some

---

[10] EA6B – An Electronic Warfare Aircraft

racial dustups, if this man's death was in any way racially motivated, this town could explode. I want a salt-and-pepper crew looking into this, and we can't rule out that he was knocked off by a local, which opens up a whole new can of worms," Tyler says.

"Look, Tyler, I'm on board, and Ricky's the best we've got, both of us like to see things through no matter which way they go," Denny says.

"Okay, Denny, you two report directly to me— no Provost Marshal or bureau glory boys—you two are my eyes and ears," Tyler says.

"Skip, we're on this like white on rice," I say.

"Okay, gents, carry on," Tyler says as we leave his office.

Denny and I go sit at his desk to go over Tyler's mandate. There were about forty agents at MIS Subic. This number was a little less than it had been before Saigon fell the previous year. The workload was hot and heavy in '75 with so many Vietnamese refugees being transited through Subic and held on Grande Island. MIS was split into three divisions; Criminal Investigations, Fraud, and Counter-Intelligence. Each division had twelve or thirteen agents and a lead agent. Denny and I, along with Tyler, were among the few prior active navy personnel assigned to Subic. Denny and Tyler were retired senior chief and lieutenant commander, respectively, I left after eight years as a first-class master at arms. Denny and I both had degrees in criminal justice.

"Ricky, we don't have a lot to sniff on this one yet. If that ID comes in positive, we can start putting this individual back together. Till then, I'll nose around VRC 45, and you check on your narcotic pals in the Ville, my brown soul brother," Denny said.

"Yeah, I got your brown soul swinging. We do need to split this detail up. Right now, it's all-hands, but if that ID comes through it might just be me and you," I say.

"Okay, you got the Ville, and I got the Naval Air Station. Let's meet at Rory's place tomorrow at 1800 and debrief over a cocktail and some *Freddy Fender*," Denny says.

"Okay, D.B., I can dig the booze, but that shit-kicking hat dance music's got to go," I say. I walk to my desk to jot down a couple notes to remind myself to talk to Doc Lefkowitz and that kid photog. I leave HQ and go to the gym to push some iron and hit the heavy bag. I've always been a gym rat and have had some of my clearest thinking after a workout.

Romeo Rodriguez, my narcotic friend Denny was referring to, was a shipmate from the Coral Sea. Romeo and I mess-cooked and coop-cleaned on the Sea in '64. I later became a master at arms thanks to a good word from RL, Papa Joe's buddy. Romeo went from shit-bird gig to shit-bird gig, all the while becoming the biggest loan shark and bookie on the carrier. He had since spread his operation to girls, black-market goods, reefer, and illegal activity in general. Romeo was the Godfather of Olongapo. He settled here after two tours in Nam, working the patrol boat riverine out of Cam Ranh Bay. He was a unique cat, five feet four inches of pure-d squatty-ass muscle — arms like pistons, and hands like bricks. He took shit from nobody. That's how we became friends. An Arkansas redneck had been fucking with me when I first went to the mess decks. He said "nigger" one too many times, and I put him in la-la land with a short right.

"Yo, homes, you a bad man. You and me, we can rule this floating shit-bucket; The Latin Soul Brothers," Romeo crowed. He was half

Filipino—his dad was a Chicano airman from Stockton, California, and his mama, a Filipina from Cebu City. He was born in Manila at the end of World War II and had dual citizenship. Romeo grew up in Northeast LA and ran with the Avenidas Gangs in the late fifties. He bragged that he had three kids by three women—one black, one brown, and one white—and about having knocked off three dudes by the time he was seventeen. He had three small teardrop tattoos by his left eye. Romeo got out of East LA and into the Navy before his past caught up with him. I'm a cop and he's a criminal. Life's funny. Romeo played both sides of the fence in Olongapo. He ran girls, gambling, and drugs, but he kept the hard stuff out of Subic Bay and was an intel conduit for the various agencies, including MIS. Because of this, he was allowed to run his brothels, clubs, and loan-sharking hassle-free. If anyone would know about China White being in Olongapo City, it would be Romeo. I'd pay him a little visit. He lived in a gated villa that he'd built in '73, it was past my place in the Barrio near Subic City, Nam had been good to him. After leaving the Navy on honorable terms with a couple Purple Hearts and a Bronze Star, he returned to his birthplace in 1971 and soon ruled the roost. He, like Papa Joe, had no plans to return to the world.

I take a Jeepney to his crib, which is surrounded by a gate. I bellowed into the intercom while looking into the black-and-white surveillance cameras, "Romeo, get your crook-ass up and get a brother a brew!" Within a minute, a heavyset, well-armed Samoan ambled out to let me in. This was Nico, Romeo's main bodyguard. He had a military .45 on his hip and an Uzi around his massive chest. Nico was about six-foot four, and 280 pounds. His legs were like tree trunks, and his hands like hams. He, too, had been in the US Navy.

"Hey, Ricardo, long time. Come on through," Nico says, opening the electric gate.

"Big Nic, good to see you, bro. You tell Romeo I'm here?" I say.

"The boss is out back. He knows you're here," Nico replies.

I walk around to the back of the crib where I find Romeo on the deck, sitting in a large Papasan chair with a small cup of coffee and a large Cuban cigar.

"Qué pasa, Capone? Am I busted, or you just want to rap about old times?"

"Homes, you know there ain't no bust between us. Give me some dap," I reply, and we dap a short time. We cross our hearts after the dap to signify we're down to kill or die for each other, if it rolls like that.

"So, Cappy, what's on your military flatfoot-assed mind?"

"Look man, we had a floater, black cat, turned up in Shit River on New Year's Eve. He had about half an ounce of pure China white up his poop chute. Who's down with that in the Ville?" I ask. About this time, a big brother, about six three, 225 pounds, with a huge 'fro and gold-tooth grin, appears with two fine bar girls clad in micro-bikinis.

"Capone, I thought I heard your jive-time squawking out here. Give the funky drummer some."

We dapped and just stared at each other, grinning. I hadn't seen Jack Gilliam— "Jabbo" to all who knew him—since 1968. Jabbo had also been on the Coral Sea with Romeo and me. He got picked up for the 7th Fleet Basketball Team in '65 and spent his whole tour with Special Services shooting hoops all over the Pacific. I'd last seen him in Da Nang when I was rotating out of Nam. Jabbo never made the NBA, but he did become a Merchant Seaman. Back on the Coral Sea, Jabbo provided Romeo with extra muscle when dudes came up short on their loans. I guess we were all tough, defiant guys in our own ways. We could be a scary sight: my scarred face, Romeo's teardrops, and Jabbo's bulk would put fear into many, but we, too were all-American kids of the fifties. Doo-wop, hot rods, and girls motivated us, just like they did any other kid. Romeo and I both grew up in LA, me near the Coliseum, and him on the east side. Our paths never crossed. Jabbo was from Chi-town. When we got thrown together on the Coral Sea, we became brothers.

"Jabbo, man, you bring me back. You and Romeo still on the gangster tip?"

"Yeah, Cap, you know black and brown don't have no way to riches, ain't no Hollywood or Wall Street for us, and I can't sing or dance. We got to take from those what's got. Dig? I make more in a month than that rooty-poot badge pays you in a year. So, go ahead and retire on your cop pay. Me, I'm done at forty years old. Look me up in Ensenada, Mexico. I'll be the Black King," Jabbo says, laughing.

"Cap here is asking about some China white that turned up on a stiff in PO Town," Romeo says.

"Hey, Cap, I'm just passing through," Jabbo says.

"Look, Mr. MIS, you know I'm a businessman, and it's in my business interests to keep that shit out of Olongapo. But anyone could bring that shit in here, from a broke-dick airdale[11], to Marcos himself. I ain't the ultimate boss here. Remember, money talks and bullshit walks. You know that, Cap," Romeo says.

"Oh, yeah, I know that well, but if you hear any scuttlebutt[12], point it my way," I say.

"Look here, Cap, if this is part of something bigger, it means some cabron is stepping on my turf, and I'll take care of it my way. Ya dig?" Romeo says.

"Right on. Do your thing, but keep me in the loop on this," I say.

Jabbo is rubbing the two girls' backsides and says, "Hey, man, fuck all this Dragnet shit. I ain't seen Cap in a minute. Let's get some more

---

[11] Airdale – Naval personnel who deal with aircrafts.
[12] Scuttlebutt – Rumer mill/grapevine

freaks and party like it's old times."

"Jabbo, man, it's noon and I got a lot of snooping left to do. I can't get bent like that this early. Give me a brew and I'll ziggy on out," I say.

Romeo gets me a frosty San Miguel and says, "Well Bro, at least dig some of the floor show," He hollers, "Senoritas!" And four more girls, just as fine as the first two, walk out, all wearing platform go-go boots. Nico puts some *James Brown* on Romeo's huge Sansui sound system, and JB screams out, "Qué pasa, people, qué pasa . . . hit me!" The stereo starts pumping that driving soul, and the girls begin to boogaloo and bump to the beat in their itty-bitty bikinis. The bikinis start to come off, and Jabbo pours champagne over their bodies, and the girls lick it off each other. I finish my brew and know I have to split before nature gets me caught up in the scene.

"Yo, y'all fellas got the American dream, but I got to work for mines. Later fellas, I'm about to duff," I say, letting Nico know I'll see myself out. *James Brown* is still thumping, and Romeo and Jabbo are in the midst of a half-dozen naked freaks. As I split, I think, "that's the young man's heaven on earth." *James Brown* wailed,

". . . the long-haired hippies and the Afro Blacks all get together across the tracks, and they PARTY."

After leaving Romeo's crib I stop by our place in the Barrio. Nea is in the kitchen making lumpia, the Filipino's version of an egg roll. She's wearing her usual house gear of cut-off Levi's and a bikini top. My nose is still open from those freaks at Romeo's place. I walk in, saying, "What's happening," kissing her neck and rubbing her rear.

She looks at me and says, "Ricky, I'm busy, you know. lumpia takes time."

I put her hand on my crotch and reply, "Baby, there's no time like the present." Nea smiles, looks me dead in the eye, and kisses me so ferociously that her tongue is damn near on my tonsils. We're naked before we reach the bed and go at each other like springtime rabbits. Afterward we light a couple of Kool's and lay back, watching the fan spin while the sweat rolls off our bodies. I start to muse about how weird this new case is: no ID, pure China white, .22 slug, and so on. I also mention that photographer, Smitty. At that, Nea remarks, "I know that guy. He married Aracele Roxas. She's a good seamstress and a fantastic designer. She makes the clothes for all the big bands."

"Wow, dig that. So, this kid's married to a local girl? That's what KC told me, too."

"Yeah, Aracele was never a street girl, just another poor girl from Santa Rita. They live right near the bridge across from Marylyn's Number One Club," Nea says, referring to a Sailor hangout notorious for its game of "smiles" - where the guys get blow jobs under the tables and have to buy beers for everybody if they smile.

I grab a beer, we sip it together, and pleasure each other some more. Afterward, we take a P.I. shower, which consists of pouring buckets of water over ourselves, soaping each other up, then rinsing off with a couple more buckets. I get dressed in my uniform of CPO khakis, and a navy-blue Cuban-style guayabera shirt. I head out the door, letting Nea know I'm going to look up Smitty and his wife. She's already back to her lumpia prep in the kitchen.

As I start walking the half mile or so to where Smitty stays, I fix on the Frogs, Ty and Derrick. I didn't mention these guys or Romeo to Nea, although she knows them all, she doesn't like dealing with any of them and considers all of them to be stone killers. She's right on that score, it is, what it is. As I approach the area where Nea told me the Smiths live, I walk into a small store and ask if a Black Sailor named Johnny Smith lives in the area. The storeowner smiles and says, "Pinsan Johnny live right up there," pointing to a small place farther up the hill. I headed up the hill thinking this Smitty must be a unique cat for that old shopkeeper to refer to him as Pinsan, which means "cousin." I get to the small hooch and knock on the open front door and an attractive, pregnant woman, about five feet five—tall for P.I.—with waist-length thick-straight hair, olive skin, great legs, and catlike eyes, asks, "Can I help you, sir?"

I ID myself and show my badge. She looks very apprehensive until I explain that Smitty did some work for us.

"Johnny with the brothers working at the new school," Aracele says.

"What!!??, some GIs got a school out here in the Barrio?"

"No, no. The brothers are Irish Monks, Johnny help them build school for local kids. He be back soon. Come in. Can I get you some iced tea?"

"Well, thanks. I won't stay long, but the tea sounds good," I say as I walk inside.

There are photos on all the walls. Large black-and-white pictures of the people and places of Subic Bay, powerful views of everyday life. There are also several mannequins with fantastic outfits on them. Aracele's designs, no doubt. I thought, when these two hit the world, New York and LA better look out.

"My lady is Nea Santos, she tells me you and Smitty are married. Is that true?"

"Yes, yes. I meet Johnny when he come to P.I. with Squadron VP 17 from Hawaii. He re-up and get stationed here so we can marry."

"Wow, I figured him as fresh out of boot camp."

"No, no, he been Sailor three years. Just no promotions for photographers in Navy," she says.

At this point, Smitty gets home and asks, "What's up, honey? Who is our guest?" He looks at me again, and I see the light of recognition on his face. "Hey, man, you that MIS fella from the autopsy, right?"

"Yeah, Bro man. That's me, Peter Gunn, but I'm also known as Special Agent Ricardo Baptiste," I shake his hand soul brother–style.

"Yeah, Photographer's Mate Airman Johnny Smith, good to know you. Am I in some trouble?"

"No, man, I just want to go over some of the details of what you saw at the autopsy before I talk to Doc Lefkowitz again."

Smitty tells me that the dope found on the body was so far up its anus that it couldn't have been inserted by the dead dude himself. He said that aside from the mutilated hands, the corpse was in a condition consistent with three to four days of decomposing in Shit River.

"Hey, honey, cervezas, please. For Mr. Baptiste," Smitty calls out.

"Hey, man, ain't no 'Mister' here. I ain't no zero. It's Ricky to my friends."

Aracele brings us a couple San Migs and some glasses with ice. We kick back and shoot the breeze for a while. Smitty has a small Kenwood system, and he puts on some *Earth, Wind & Fire* and *"Head to the Sky"* fills the small crib. As I look at Smitty and Aracele, or "Celi," as she's called, I can see the love and happiness between them. Both very talented, yet very humble, almost shy. Smitty is six foot one, but only about 170 pounds. He is well muscled through the shoulders and upper body, with medium-brown skin, short hair with a part on the left—Muslim-style—and prescription aviators. I figure him for hoops, probably a point guard.

"Hey, man, Chief Street tells me you're from Philly or Jersey, said you know your way around a camera, too."

"Well, I grew up in Minneapolis, but I played a little baseball in Jersey, instructional league—good in the field, but couldn't hit the pitching even at that level," Smitty says, while tapping his aviators. "I moved across the river to the Big Apple to pursue my other love, photography. Had a grant at the New School for a semester, ran out of dough so I got into the Navy's Photo Program. I know my craft, but the photogs don't welcome brothers with open arms. It's been an uphill fight, especially here in P.I."

"Yeah, your Senior Chief Deforest, is a stone-to-the-bone bigot. Archie Bunker don't have shit on that SOB," I reply.

Smitty tells me about his and Celi's work with

fashion and photography, and with the Missionaries' School—how he helped build it and Celi teaches sewing and prepares meals for the kids with excess food he gets from the base.

"You two are a breath of Spring air. After doing this gig here for a while, you get really jaded, y'all have given me some hope," I say. "It was a pleasure to meet you. I may have Manny make a few more prints, and I might need to talk to you again."

"You're welcome here anytime, Mr. Ricky," Smitty says.

At this, Smitty and I shake hands, and Celi gives me a little hug. I wave good-bye and start back down the hill thinking to myself maybe this world isn't all dog-eat-dog. Here are two people in love and spreading love in Olongapo P.I., of all places.

Meanwhile, Denny B was sitting in the Squadron CO's office with autopsy pictures of the John Doe floater.

"That could be Goins, but the face is so decomposed, it's hard to tell. Hell, most coloreds look about alike to me anyway," the CO says with a slight smirk.

"All the same Captain, maybe you could give

me a rundown on his service jacket," Denny says.

The CO informs Denny that Goins was on a six-month TAD from a squadron in Miramar; his orders had come straight from the Commander, US Pacific Fleet. "That young man was supposed to be a top Aviation Electrician (AE), with regards to the EA6B. He was assigned here to help train our E5 and E6 AE's on the quirks of that aircraft. He worked with Miller and Le Croix over in Aircraft Maintenance Department. I'll call over and let them know you'll be talking with them. I'm sure they can give you more insight than me," the CO flatly stated, sensing his racial remark hadn't sat too well with old Denny B.

When Denny got to the Maintenance Department Miller and Le Croix were waiting for him in Miller's office. Like Denny, they were both white men in their early to mid-forties, all seemingly cut from the same cloth. When Denny showed the pictures to the men, both said it was possible that it was Goins, but that Phil Goins was slim and had short hair.

"You know when Mac and that other twidget Zimmerman brought this kid to train us, I copped an attitude big-time. What the hell's this spade going to tell me about aircraft? But that kid knew his stuff, had a degree from one of those colored Colleges in Ohio somewhere. He was an outstanding AE and a clean-cut kid. He got my respect," Le Croix said. Miller echoed Le Croix's remarks. Denny then asked about Goins' personal habits.

"From what I could see, this guy was AJ squared aware; didn't smoke, rarely even tipped a beer, and he was married with a couple of kids back in CONUS," Miller said.

"But he did run with that tech rep Zimmerman, they had some rooms at the Royal. I heard Goins had a big tall hooker that was built like Sophia Loren, I shit you not," Le Croix added.

"So, you're saying that Goins hung with these twidgets and shacked up at the Royal on their dime?" Denny asked.

"No, he and Zim ran together, not Mac. Mac did his drinking on base, even had a little girlfriend worked at the FRA Bar. Mac's been in and out of P.I. for years," Le Croix said.

"Well, what about this Zimmerman?" Denny asked.

"Zim was a P.I. cherry boy[13]. Mac said he was a bean counter from their HQ in New York sent to check on his shit. They didn't get along very well. Smart-ass hippie college boy, big red Afro, John Lennon glasses, smug, and full of shit. Didn't know squat about aircraft. Hell, his daddy probably plays golf with the manufacturer's CEO. He liked to party, always had some fine hookers around him and would bring a GI a can full of San Migs for rope yarn every Wednesday," Le Croix said, grinning at the thought. He added, "Sumbitch said his hookers were 'prime tenderloin groin'—that guy was a rounder in anyone's book."

"When did the tech reps leave VRC?" Denny asked.

Miller replied, "they both went back stateside after Thanksgiving, maybe early December, but Goins caught P.I. fever and took a thirty-day leave here. Guess that big doll blew his military mind. He was due to rotate to the Naval Air Station in Memphis, only had about a year left on his hitch—was gonna be a tech rep himself. Sure hope that picture isn't Phil."

---

[13] Cherry boy - Virgin

CHAPTER 4

As I'm walking down the hill, I see Jackson double-timing it down the road toward my place. I call out to him. "Yo, little brother, where you bookin' to?"

Jackson says, "Denny B say meet at Rory Club *di di mao,"* He used the Vietnamese term we all use that means "Get a move on,"

"When did you talk to Denny?" I ask.

"At my Uncle's pop stand. He already smell drunk."

Denny was a juicer and never claimed otherwise. Beer was like soda pop for him, and he always had a flask of C.C.—Canadian club—on him, day or night. I drank hard myself, and still smoked a little reefer or hash on occasion. But neither vice had become a habit with me yet. Luckily, Denny's boozing didn't detract from his powers of detection.

"Come on, little bro, let's catch up with Denny," I say as we get into a Jeepney that takes us from the barrio back to the Victory Liner Station in Olongapo, which is very near KC's crib and the Hotel Royal. I make a mental note that I have some ground to cover there. I give Jackson twenty pesos, and hop a trike headed to the main gate. It's 1500 hours and traveling down Rizal Street I can see the parade of life in this third-world GI town; early morning hookers with and without sailors, little markets and pop stands, money changers, BBQ sellers cooking their chicken, beef, or monkey meat out in the open, and Beer Gardens, restaurants, and clubs with music and street noise all assaulting the senses at once. *Rico Puno*, the Filipino soul man, rises above the din with his covers of the *Temptations and the Dells*. At the same time, the betting is fast and furious at the back-alley cockfights, money changing hands faster than the eye can see. Papa Joe and his prize bird, Big Red, are taking on all challengers and kicking much tail. I'm thinking there are a million and one stories in this buck-naked village.

"Put your cash up and give it up. I got Big Red the barnyard pimp here, and he's gonna make your birds punk-assed hens. Give it up!" Papa Joe boasts. Joe and Nea's Uncle, Ernie, have been breeding these birds for years and they're killing machines. Today they'll clear about a thousand US dollars.

Back in the jungle, past the Harlem and ghetto clubs, behind some small hovels, Starchild, the transvestite Benny boy is talking to several other Benny boys and hookers while washing clothes using a scrub board and an old-fashioned wringer. Lettie, a hooker with a lot of jungle time, warns him, "Some brother no like Benny boy surprise. You go Baclat Club, 7th is no good for you"

Starchild replies that he can take care of himself, and adds, "a lot of 'straight' GI like it both ways, and they pay better than stone faggots."

"Okay, Starchild, you keep messing with soul brothers, you gonna see," Lettie states flatly.

At the Duck Pin Bowling Alley, below the Foxy Brown Club, Jackson and two of his pals are drinking pop cola and rolling the little duck balls at the small pins. Jackson plays big shot with the twenty p - I gave him. "I'm secret-agent man like Denny B and Ricky. I get out P.I. soon, go to world—LA, man. I be superstar in LA," Jackson crows to his boys who marvel at his dealings with the American GIs.

Past Gordon Street, near the Shit River, the tall, bald officer is giving some dresses and a Barbie doll to a slender young girl of about ten or eleven, who is over-whelmed with joy and excitement. The bald man winks at the Mamasan and says, "This one is fine. I want her on Friday." He hands the Mamasan a C-note. "I'll pay the rest on Friday,"

In the back room of the Club Viking, a group of seven or eight White Sailors and a couple of Marines are giving the Nazi salute and repeating, "White power! White power!" Their leader, a big, muscular burr-headed dude, is preaching: "The sub-humans are taking over our country. These gooks are here to service our needs, but no real white man should ever mate and reproduce mongrelized bastards with these little monkeys. We must keep them out of our homeland. The war is over. We got no need for those mud people living on our tax dollars in the homeland. Niggers are for shining our boots, cleaning our heads, cooking our chow, and doing our dying." The diatribe would continue for quite a while, interrupted only by shouts of "White power! White power!"

At Rory's Club, the Nueva Filipina, Denny B sat nursing a C.C. and Coke, and listening to "*El Paso City*" by *Marty Robbins,* while waiting for me with the first real break in our case. He and his lady, Rory, talk about the old fleet in the fifties before Nam. This is when they'd met and

Aurora—or Rory—was still a beautiful P.I. bar girl, even as she was pushing past forty.

"Out in the West Texas town of El Paso, I fell in love with a Mexican girl . . ," Denny nursed his drink as the country-and-western tune finished. The music then went back to Nueva's regular fare of *Sinatra, Mathis, Laine,* and the like. This bar catered to old-timers, lifers, and retirees of the World War II and Korea generation. This was Denny's sanctuary, and its owner, Rory, was his steady lady. Denny had three grown kids back in CONUS, and a wild-ass teenage son, Tommy, who we all called "Peanuts," after the comic strip. Peanuts lived on base but was out in Olongapo chasing tail and drinking as much as any squid on liberty. Hell, he was seventeen years old—might as well make hay while the sun shines. Rory also had kids—two grown girls who lived in the States. Both were nurses, Rory paid for their education at Manila University. Not bad for a P.I. bar girl. Rory was around forty-three or forty-four years old, but still a knockout. Tall for a Filipino at five foot seven, with thick, stylishly cut hair, and always dressed in the high-collar, brightly colored silky, sexy, elegant Chinese fashion. She and Denny went back to the 1950s and

had settled into a comfortable groove together. An older version of Nea and me. I was like an Uncle to Peanuts, and a little brother to Rory. Rory's English was flawless America West Coast due to several years living in Tacoma, Washington, with her late husband, an army dude.

"You know, baby, this floater is going to be a real wild hair for me and Ricky. At least now we've got a name, but this whole scene is wrong. A black kid like this guy just don't end up in Shit River," Denny mused.

"Honey-co, anything can and will happen in Olongapo. He turned up dead because he was into some bad stuff—dope, black market, whatever. He crossed the line too many times," Rory says and adds, "I bet another GI knocked him off."

"You know, my life was a lot easier when I was just an AFP cheating on my wife and taking kickbacks," Denny laughs.

"Yeah, Mr. Denny, but how many of us other women were you cheating on too?" Rory asks.

"Too many to keep track of. That's why I set my hindquarters right here with the finest piece of brown tail in the P.I.," Denny says.

"Okay, honey, just make sure your old ass can handle all this here," Rory says, patting her rear end. "Come here guapo and give Mommy a kiss, I know you can handle this stuff I got." Rory says as I walk in winking at Denny.

As I walk in, *Sinatra* is wailing with *Count Basie*. *"Come Fly With Me"* fills the air, and Denny and Rory are howling with laughter. There are five or six other older guys there, along with three mature bar girls.

"Okay, soul brother, don't think you're hot shit. You're still just a scar-faced scumbag," Denny says to me.

"Yeah, Papasan, I may be a scumbag to you, but your daughter still calls me Daddy-O," I say.

"Look here, I'm all for integration, just not with my daughters. Me and you is integrated enough."

"So, what's up, Denny? I thought tomorrow was the meet day."

"Well, Tyler got confirmation that the stiff was indeed AE1 Phillip Goins. The Bureau guys matched his dental records."

Denny went on to describe his VRC visit, and how by all accounts Goins was Mr. AJ squared-away squid, even the redneck Command Senior Chief spoke well of him. As he talked, things that stuck out in my mind were his relationship to tech rep Zimmerman, and those big girls they were seen with. It was rare for a Filipina to be more than five foot six or seven, even those of mixed blood. But the dames were supposedly five ten or better—fashion-model height. Also staying at the Royal was unusual. Most tech reps stayed in the BOQ or the Navy Lodge on base. The Royal was a first-class joint, the only one in Olongapo, but it was fifty US dollars a night, enough pesos for four or five hookers in a regular P.I. flophouse. The Royal was also where mercs like the Frogs and other Government spooky types, shacked up while in Po-town. This case seemed to get heavier by the minute.

"What you think, boss man? Looks like we need to run down those twidgets and check out the Royal," I say.

"Those techs went back to CONUS after Thanksgiving, but MacMillan was an old P.I. hand. He might be back by now," Denny says.

"Well, let's just stay status quo, you on base and me in the Ville," I suggest.

"You know that's why I like you, Ricky. We're on the same wavelength—you know, great minds and all. Hey, baby, freshen Ricky's Jack up and put on some *Buck Owens* or *Hank Snow*. This goombah shit is killing me. I don't know what's worse—wops or spades—but together it's too much for my military mind," Denny says.

Rory hooks me up with my drink, and I look Denny dead in the eye and say, "Hey DB, eat shit and die, you redneck mother."

All three of us crack up.

CHAPTER 5

My investigation over the next few days had turned up info that connected the name Phillip Goins with the body that had washed up on the banks of Shit River, it had me looking at this case in a different light. Here was a sailor who was about my age and married with a couple of young kids. An Aviation Electrician First Class, who apparently was tops in his field—a field that had very few blacks, which meant he must have been super sharp. To top that off, he hardly smoked or drank. It made no sense to me that a squared-away family man like Phillip Goins would leave his family for some tall Asian tail and be running China white on the side.

At HQ, we were getting a line on his wife and kids, and his finances. The kids, two girls ages seven and eleven years old, were staying with Goins' mother in Cleveland, Ohio. His finances were very flush, in the few months he was in P.I. he sent fifteen thousand dollars extra to his wife back in San Diego. Now, his wife was a different story, seems like she was having a hot-and-heavy with a marine, and might have "Dear Johned" Goins. After splitting from California, she took the kids back to Ohio, dropped them and a couple grand off on

Grandma, and has been on the lam ever since. Looks like her Jody wouldn't leave his happy home, so she was off doing her thing on Goins' dime. These revelations just confounded the case more. That amount of cash going home definitely gave the impression that Goins had another line of work besides aircraft maintenance. If his wife did Dear John him, it might have really fucked with Goins' military mind, but the fact that she split might mean they were running this dope thing down as a team. I was writing up some notes when Tyler called Denny and me into his office.

"Gents, this Goins case looks like it's getting deeper by the minute. It's only been forty-eight hours since Goins was positively ID'd. His mom was just notified yesterday, and his old lady up and vanished. I want some thoughts and theories. We need to get this one off our books ASAP. I have a hunch that there's a real can of worms here. What you fellas got for me?"

"Well, Skip," Denny says, "the boys at VRC swear Goins walked on water. Best aircraft man to come down the pike for a while. Not only a wrench man, but a guy that could engineer and design. They took it real hard when I verified his death to them yesterday.

The AIMD[14] locker was damn near having a wake for him."

I throw my two cents in. "I snooped around out in the Ville. Seems like Romeo and crew had no direct connection to Goins or the China white. I also snooped around the Royal, and that joint was the boogie-down with the tech rep Zimmerman the MC."

"How so, Rick?" Tyler asks.

"Well, it seems like Zim, as he was called, rented a group of rooms on one corner of the top floor, paid ninety days in advance—fourteen thousand US dollars. Had two big tall hookers with him, Layla and Nita, both about five foot nine. Goins was a regular guest and spent many nights with Layla. The doormen and the maids felt these women were Chinese or maybe Korean. They claimed to have heard them and Zimmerman speaking Chinese, and Goins called his gal Me Li sometimes. Our boy Zim partied hearty, would have a lot of booze, reefer, and extra local talent up in his roost."

"Okay, Rick, I get your drift. This guy Zimmerman was running some kind of scam, and dragged our man Goins in," Tyler says.

---

[14] AIMD – Aircraft Intermediate Maintenance Department

"I don't know how it went down, Skip. The hotel folks figured they were making pornos. But all types of American civilians and a few of Marcos' boys were in and out. My man Romeo, and Ty and Deke were also visitors at least a couple of times," I say.

"Goddamn, the Black Frogs!? Well, they didn't knock Goins off or he'd be short an eye. In fact, wouldn't be a body left to ID," Denny says.

"Well that's a fact Jack," Tyler says, echoing what we all knew from our time in Cam Ranh Bay—that when the Frogs took out a target, it was often with a shot through the left eye. This calling card made them the most feared snipers in Vietnam, but they could also dispose of bodies without a trace, if need be. So, it seems unlikely that they knocked Goins off.

"Gentlemen, this ruse that Zimmerman was running out of the Royal had some heavy players in and out. This case could reach up into the higher echelons, in which case the heroes from the agencies will bigfoot us off it. So, let's try to get a line on this one, pronto," Tyler said.

I'd started to develop some hunches on the case when the killing of some Philippine

Nationals on the Navy MAG[15] outside of Cubi Point NAS[16] took our attention away from it for a while. Because of a rise in goods being ripped off from the bases, and weakened security in general, the US forces contracted with a group of indigenous Filipinos known as Negritos to provide perimeter security for the bases. The leader of these men was Roberto Sosa, a tribal chieftain. These men also trained US personnel in jungle survival. I had trained with them, and so had most MIS agents. Roberto and his crew were the true people of the P.I.: short, compact, and muscular, with thick, curly black hair and deep-brown skin. They had been here before the Malay, Chinese, Spanish, Japanese, and Americans ran roughshod over this land and intermixed with its people. These men were perfectly adapted to it, they could exist in their jungle homes with no more than their trusty bolo knives. They were also ruthlessly efficient military operatives, much like Gurkhas or Montagnards. This time it seems that Roberto's crew popped four nationals who had trespassed onto base territory. This quickly turned into an all-hands effort for the Criminal Division. We also had a couple of guys from

---

[15] Navy Mag – Naval Magazine, a storage area for bombs
[16] NAS – Naval Air Station

fraud working on this as well. The shit hit the fan because of a newspaper article that cited this as more evidence that the United States should be out of P.I. The Olongapo Mayor, Mr. Horton, was also raising all kinds of hell, but he was a stooge for Uncle Sam right from the get-go. His ranting was more of an act for the people. In any case, we needed to quell this shit ASAP.

There was a large garbage dump at the edge of Cubi Point NAS. All the refuse, crates, containers, and unwanted surplus of this huge military facility ended up at this site. There were several acres of boxes that once held Frigidaire's and Kenmore's, huge pieces of wood that had housed military equipment, and even some junked American and Japanese cars. There were also the people—hundreds of the poorest of the poor—living in the garbage of the superpower inside the crates and boxes and abandoned vehicles of America. These were entire families: moms, pops, and kids. Third world and first world colliding. I thought I'd seen poverty, especially in the dirt roads and tarpaper shacks of my pop's home state of South Carolina, and in Tijuana and its outskirts, but it was nothing like what I'd seen as a Sailor in places like Karachi, Pakistan, or here in P.I. These people were the wretched of the earth. Unlike the poor in the first world, who were producers and consumers in the capitalist system, these folks produced nothing and bought little. They were surplus humans in the grand scheme of money, profit, and plunder. As Denny and I approach the dump, we see Roberto and two of his men standing near it.

"*Como estaka*, Robby?" Denny hollers as we approach the men.

"Brother Denny, cousin Ricardo, welcome! Let's talk," Roberto says in very clipped English.

"What exactly went on out there, Robby?" Denny asks.

"Our orders say stop all trespassers who are outside of this garbage town. We arrest, detain, and turn over to the Provost Marshal and PC. But these men shot at us, so we return fire and kill two men, not four, as was reported."

"Shot at you with what?" I ask.

"M-14 rifles. They were rear guard of a larger platoon. They didn't know jungle and couldn't shoot good in the dark."

"Platoon? What the hell you talkin' about Robby?" Denny asks.

"These two hung back at the perimeter of NAVMAG. We find many footprints—fifteen sets, maybe more—horse prints, and sled tracks—somebody steal big from base," Robby says.

"So, what you're saying is an organized group is stealing large items from base and bringing them out through the jungle?" I ask.

"I don't know what they take. We turned the rifles and bodies over to the Provost. We found nothing else until a couple hours ago," Robby says, and waves his hand, pointing to something wrapped in a blanket.

Two of his men lay it at our feet and unwrap it. It's a bent gray pipe that looks like it might have come off a truck. Denny and I thank Robby. We pick the pipe up and take it back to the photo lab to have some flicks made of it and to look over the negs from the Goins autopsy to see if those scratch marks meant anything. Maybe an extreme blowup would tell. I got to the photo lab at about 1700 hours. The shop was closed, but Manny was at the duty desk in the front of the building. Smitty and a PH3 were also in this duty section. Smitty, had been given another shit detail, burning photographic materials and reclaiming the silver it yielded. It was a long process that took place within the burn cage, which contained a mini blast furnace. It was already hot in P.I., but this furnace generated an unbearable degree of heat. He was in the cage in a skivvy shirt drenched with sweat.

"What it is, Smitty!" I holler.

"Same shit, different day," Smitty replies.

"I heard that, bro," I say as I duck into the photo lab and head over to Manny. After greeting each other, I run down what I need done.

"Have Smitty take a few shots of this pipe from several angles. Black and white is fine. Give me five, eight by tens of the best angles. Get close-ups of any numbers or writing on this thing, put it on the MIS ticket. Also, I was hoping that we could take a closer look at the autopsy photos of Goins."

"Goins was that guy's name? I been thinking about him since I made the prints," Manny says.

"Yeah, AEI Phillip Goins, thirty-two years old,

from Ohio," I say.

"Okay, Ricky, let's take a closer look at the stuff," Manny says. We go into his darkroom. I hand him the negs, and we look at them on a light table. We find two frames that show the marks. Manny hikes the enlarger way up till the small scratches almost fill the eight-by-ten frame.

"Man, I don't know what this shit is, Ricky. Looks like chicken scratch to me."

"Let's make some prints and see what it looks like in color."

The prints are finished in about half an hour. As I look at the finished color prints, I can see that the scratches are just random scars. When I'd been looking at the negs back at HQ, I thought I could make out the Nazi swastika symbol. Just wishful thinking I guess, hoping that I'd found a rationale as to why Goins got offed, but a racially motivated hit was seeming more and more unlikely.

CHAPTER 6

The USS Constellation CV64, "The Connie," is steaming toward P.I., it's due to tie up in Subic Bay early in the day. Channel fever, the expectation of P.I. hookers and San Miguel beer, has the crew all wound up. In the CPO the mess cooks are preparing midrats - midnight rations - so chiefs can get a meal at any time. A couple of old, salty chiefs are laughing about leaving their families in San Diego and returning to their loved ones in P.I. Two cooks, with P.I. experience, are telling two cherry-boy cooks what the real deal is in Olongapo City.

"Look, fellas, this ain't Yokosuka. This is Olongapo City, P.I., I mean party time all the time. These dames down here will fuck you any which way you want for three US dollars. I shit you not," says Renda, a Second-Class MS from the Bronx, New York. The two mess cooks—a farm boy from South Dakota named Dawson and Hinton, a black kid from Tulsa, Oklahoma, are on their first West PAC and are cherry boys to the P.I.

"Yeah, even two L-Seven[17] hayseeds like you

---

[17] L-Seven - Square

two can get it on with any stone fox you want, because you got *peso*-nality. That means your bullshit E-2 pay is long green over here," adds MS3 Johnson, a twenty-five-year-old Black Sailor from Detroit.

The two boot camps are taking information in with wide-eyed disbelief. Dawson is only seventeen, and the Navy has been his first time away from South Dakota. Hinton is a couple years older and has been around the block, but Olongapo is a whole new bag.

Johnson keeps on with his travelogue, "Look, Dawson, you white boys got two streets; the main drag - that's got all the Rock and Roll music and beer you want, all that Lynyrd Skynyrd shit y'all dig and a little shit kickin' side street with Country and Western bars. Just keep your snowball asses out the jungle, that's brother turf."

"Yeah, let the brothers keep their jungle. We got the best-looking broads and boss bands on the main drag. That fucking jungle is a sideshow," Renda says.

Just keep your freak ass out of my sideshow, goombah. You dig?" Johnson snorts.

"MS3 Johnson, I find your remark ethnically

offensive. You hurt my feelings," Renda says, mimicking the racial-understanding courses the Navy had instituted in recent years.

"I got your feelings swinging," Johnson says, grabbing his crotch. All four men crack up laughing. "By this time tomorrow, I'll be dancing with the prettiest piece of ass in P.I.," Johnson goes on.

"Yeah, while you're dancing, I'll be fucking for free. I'm gonna get me an ugly dame and give her some of our good CPO chow, and I'll be balling free this whole port call," Renda says with a wink at the mess cooks.

Back in the print shop, the LI's are having their usual dispute about the sounds being played. They're fed up with the loud, hard rock of *"Freebird."*

"Yo, yo, yo, you square motherfuckers got to quell this shit," one LI says, as he pops out the Skynyrd and drops *Funky Nassau* into the boom box. The band starts jamming: *"Nassau's gone funky, Nassau's gone soul,"* him and his cohort start grooving to the beat and using garbage cans as conga drums. A skinny white boy from Waco, hollers, "Man, fair's fair, but this boogie shit's got to go."

"Man, fuck you in your redneck ass! Tomorrow we'll all be in P.I., and you can listen to them Asian brothers play that '*Freebird*' all day long. Just try to dig our scene for a minute, and by the way, let's turn two on getting this shop policed up for inspection," says the night-shift LPO[18].

Since Saigon fell in April of 1975, there has only been one carrier group in Subic at a time, but still over five thousand sailors with a pocket full of cash and hard-ons had Olongapo geeked up to high gear. "Welcome Connie" banners lined the main drag, and the High Plains Club sent its number one band and some bad go-go dancers to greet the ship as it pulled into its berth. Liberty call started at 1000 hours for the Connie Sailors not standing duty. It's still early, even by P.I. standards, but the squids are already hitting the beach in earnest through the main gate where the Marine and Provost Marshal guards counted every military head. The shore patrol from the battle group was heavy, everyone expecting some shit on the first night in Olongapo City. A lot of cherry boys will be P.I. qualed this day.

While in port the Connie, like most carriers,

---

[18] LPO – Lead Petty Officer

went to six-section duty so the squids could get the maximum P.I., R&R; the Sailors and Marines were all wound up like kids on Christmas Eve. Even the lamest, ugliest, square from L-Seven-ville could be balling with a fine hammer or two by sundown. Once out of the gate, it's just a short walk over the Shit River Bridge, into Disneyland Far East, a Sailor's wet dream come true. Renda, Johnson, Dawson, Hinton, and the mess cooks from the CPO are crossing the Bridge, headed to never-never land. The cherry boys are taking in the sights, sounds, and stench of PO Town for the first time. As soon as they reached the bridge, they see the Bonka Boat Queens begging for pesos while the ten and twelve-year-old boy daredevils dive into the refuse-filled river to grab the coins that the girls' nets miss.

"Man, did you catch that little dude swan-dive into that mess?" Hinton asks, commenting on one of the kid high divers who swan-dive for pesos that fall into the cesspool.

"Look here, Boot Camp, you won't even remember that shit by tomorrow," Johnson says.

"Okay, fellas, first round is on me, then I'm taking Dawson down on Gordon Street. You soul brothers can roam your jungle," Renda says. The four stop at a beer/pop stand just over the bridge and Renda, true to his word buys a round, then Johnson buys one, after which Renda collars his charge, Dawson.

"C'mon Boot, we're getting you a P.I. haircut," Renda says, winking at Johnson.

"Brothers are more suave than that. I'm taking Hinton for a rub-and-tug at the Swedes," Johnson answers.

"Right on," Renda laughs as the four down their brews and part company.

On Gordon Street the tall Commander with the ramrod-straight military bearing and many medals, awards and citations attesting to his bravery and leadership, is walking to his rendezvous. At forty-four years of age, he is the poster child of the all-American husband, father, war hero, country-clubbing, martini-sipping suburbanite. His family back in California is typical middle-class; two teenage girls in college running wild on his dime, and a Navy Officer's wife spending everything else. He's a by-the-book, hard-ass, XO of his VP squadron, who is viewed with respectful contempt by his men. The Commander has a secret itch that he can scratch for a small sum in the third-world ports that the 7th Fleet hits. He likes girls, like most GIs, but he likes them young and underdeveloped; ten and twelve-year-olds are perfect, and these little Asian girls are so smooth, and hairless. He has molested girls of every race, color, and creed worldwide, always paying for his activities in poor third-world locations from Mexico to Kenya. His own daughters were lucky they took after his mother and were tall and stacked, wearing bras at ten years old. Fat cows to him, unlike his stick-thin wife who he demanded keep herself hairless. Today the Commander will spend time with his new baby doll, an eleven-year-old hooker who looks all of eight or nine. He has met her and given her Mamasan the green light, today is the first time they'll be alone. He'll go slow with her—a kiss, a lick, rub her body with baby oil, and if she's not too scared, maybe even expose himself to her. To facilitate this, he has brought some dolls and clothes from the Navy Exchange, even some pesos to give directly to her. If things go well, he'll pay the Mamasan top dollar for her, a hundred US a shot. He throws the book out the window when it comes to his personal obsession over sex with young girls. He's had a couple problems in the past, but nothing some greenbacks and the US Navy couldn't smooth over.

Emilio Berrio was getting his female gear together. With the Constellation in port he'll have his pick of cherry boys who aren't hip to Benny boys. Lette, one of his housemates warns him, "Starchild, you not know soul brothers. They not like Benny boy surprise. They find that little ding-a-ling and its number ten big time. You stay in Baclat Bar, not 7th Heaven."

Emilio flashes a smile, and with a quicksilver motion of his hand, opens a razor-sharp butterfly knife. "Remember, Emilio was slickee boy before he become Benny boy," he slyly asserts.

"You still watch out, Starchild, soul brother real violent with Benny boy." That's Lette's final warning. They continue to discuss their outfits and speculate on what kind of new dance steps the brothers would bring from the world.

Meanwhile, Denny was nosing around the redneck joints on Gordon Street looking into a possible racial motivation for Goins' death. He was in VP Alley, a club that catered to the flyboys from the P3 squadrons who deploy to P.I. six months at a whack. VP Alley's character didn't change drastically, even with a carrier battle group in port. It's known fleet wide for one old World War II–era hooker called Mumbles, who had about as many teeth as a duck, but gave the best head in Olongapo. All the fucking new-guy cherry boys from the VP squadrons had to get "Mumbles qualed," which meant having the old hag go down on them, and the poor flyboy better stay aroused or he'd be known as "Broke Dick Airman" for his entire VP career. There's a good little crowd in the Alley, and Denny is among them, sipping a C.C. and throwing darts. His playing partner is an old Master Chief from VP 22, AOCM Bugsy Morrel.

"Denny boy, you still got that eagle eye. I ain't giving you no more of my hard, stolen pay," Bugsy laments.

"Bugs, it's not the eye, it's the wrist. I've been telling you that for twenty years. How much longer you boys in P.I.?" Denny asks.

"Man, we just got here a couple weeks back. Got another five and a half months in sailor heaven. I'm getting the roundest, firmest, fullest-packed dame in this Ville and giving her all my per diem. This is my last run, Denny. I'll be joining you sand crabs after this do-si-do."

"Well, congrats, Bugs. What you got, thirty-five or more?"

"That's it, pard. Went in summer of '41, just before Pearl Harbor. You were still a pup back then."

"Yeah, well, you had a hell of a ride. Hey, Bugs, what you know about that Club Viking down the street?" Denny asks.

"Well, I heard they don't care for niggers there, but hell, we don't like 'em too much in the alley either. Why you askin'?"

"A Black Sailor turned up dead awhile back. Looks like it could be foul play, so we're looking at all angles. Maybe it was a racial thing," Denny says.

"Denny, very few coloreds are in the VP community. The few that we've got seem to be pretty sharp, mostly college boys. They're better educated than the whites. I'm old Navy, I'm used to coloreds as cooks and stewards. It's hard to take 'em serious as AOs or ETs, but that's what that fucking Zummie's equal-opportunity new Navy has created."

"Hey, Bugs, if a man can do a job, what's skin color got to do with it? Take your head out your ass and look around. It's a new day," Denny says.

"Denny, in my head I know you're right, but my heart just won't buy it. I'm from Pittsburgh, and we don't burn many crosses up there. We just want the colored to stay in their place. Now that Club Viking is for them good ol' stars-and-bars boys, but I don't think those Southern boys would snuff another Sailor—colored or not. But who knows? And I really don't give a rat's ass. Denny, you're free, white, and twenty-one, so go on down the street and check the Viking for yourself."

"Yeah, Bugs, I might just do that. But look here, the civilian world is changing, too, so you might as well get used to seeing Blacks and even women in new roles, maybe even as your boss. Remember, life, liberty, and all the rest are what we've been protecting for all these years. The government is saying it's not just for the white man, but for all Americans. It's a different U S of A, Bugs, and you're becoming a dinosaur fast," Denny says, laying some truth on the old Master Chief.

Although in outward appearance and manner of speech, Dennis Bartholomew King was your classic Okie from Muskogee, shit-kicking, beer-lapping, *Hank Snow*–listening redneck. A good ol' boy who often spoke in demeaning terms of minorities and women, as did most sailors. The difference with Denny was that it was 90 percent pure acting. In reality, Denny wasn't even American. He was born and raised in Nova Scotia by Quaker parents. His dad died when he was five or six years old, but his mom raised him and his siblings, with her all-people-are-God's-children philosophy. Blacks had gone to Nova Scotia prior to the US Civil War via the Underground Railroad and had firmly established communities there. Denny went to sea on fishing boats as a teenager, and the man who showed him the ropes was a Black First Mate named Flannigan. Denny claimed he was the truest man God ever made. So, after coming south to the good ol' USA, he never bought into its racist claptrap, although he wasn't above parroting it to his own advantage. Old Denny B sauntered into the Club Viking and bellowed, "Can a white man get a drink in here without smelling a bunch of niggers and listening to that Jigaboo jungle noise?"

The crowd inside laughed, and a huge burr-head marine said, "Welcome, my Aryan brother, to your home in this armpit of the world. The only niggers here are these slope-headed monkeys that service our manly needs," said Staff Sergeant Ron Alston.

The clubs on the main drag, Magsaysay Boulevard, were jamming hard. The Connie Sailors were flush with ducats after thirty-two days on the water. Their previous port call had been Yokosuka, Japan, which offered few of the P.I.'s affordable amenities. Japan was fast becoming a first-world economic power, and consequently, the Japanese women didn't sell booty at bargain-basement prices. Now that didn't mean you couldn't pull any tail up there; you just had to do it in the old-fashioned way— with a roll of cash, or rap and style. The young Japanese women loved soul brothers' rap and style. Many squids were just shit out of luck in Yokosuka and spent a little cash at the enlisted men's clubs on and around the base, and those little dives on the Honcho strip. Many saved their cash for P.I., and some real liberty. Olongapo was a whole different bag. There were ten thousand ready and willing, poverty-stricken young women anxious to do whatever it took to separate the GIs from their greenbacks. In P.I., a poor boy could live like a millionaire, if only for a day or two. Rich dudes can buy their fine tail worldwide, but the poor Sailor boy has P.I., and for real - it don't get much better than liberty call in PO Town with a pocket full of dough.

The High Plains Club was about to explode. The band and their star guitarist, Enrique Paz, were in a Clapton set: *"Badge," "Layla,"* and a thirty-minute jam of *"Sunshine of Your Love."* The twenty bikini-clad dancers were rocking all the way out, the sweat glistening on their tight, brown bodies. The young, mostly white sailors were going apeshit. These were the best-looking girls on the main drag, and the band was smoking hot. Close your eyes and *Eric, Jack,* and *Ginger* were right there. The thirty waitresses in their black cocktail miniskirts and platform heels couldn't keep the San Miguels and ladies' drinks coming fast enough. Every dame in the joint was a China doll, a Sailor's wet dream for sale or rent. Much cash and body fluid would be exchanged via the High Plains this night.

Down the street at the corner of Magsaysay and Rizal Street where the 7th Heaven Club stood, was where the black side of town, known as the "Jungle," started. The Jungle clubs were first-floor joints, most with just a jukebox and bar, with names like Birdland and Freedman's. There were two large dance halls, the Harlem and the Ghetto, that boasted live bands, but the 7th Heaven was the boss joint with the baddest hammers. It was set up like a main-drag club with a nightclub on the second floor. Inside the 7th, a DJ was spinning *Van McCoy's "Hustle,"* and the dancers were getting off. As the song ended, the band came out—six Filipinos and three Black GIs - who roared into *"Hollywood Swinging."* The crowd was frenetic, and the shouts of "Shit!" "Goddamn!" and "Git off your ass and jam" were raising the roof. The black lights and strobes made the scene more surreal. Any stateside brother who hadn't been in Southeast Asia before couldn't wrap his dome around P.I. The music, booze, women, and partying were so good, cheap, and readily available that cats figured they'd died and gone to players' heaven, and the 7th was damn near Shangri-la. Johnson, the P.I. Vet and his cherry-boy charge, Hinton, were sitting in the 7th drinking with Johnson's girl, Baby Black. Baby is a Filipina who has the body of a soul sister: big round ass, full breasts, and thick, shapely legs. The brothers wig when they see that package on a China-doll face. For that reason, Baby picks and chooses her men. Johnson is her Connie sailor, he shells out twenty US dollars a night for her company instead of the twenty pesos for a regular hooker.

"Look here, Lil Black, this square is my shipmate bro, Hinton. He's cherry to the P.I., so hook him up with something good," Johnson says.

Lewis is eyeballing Starchild, who's dancing with a tall light-skinned dude.

"That no good for you sailor. That Benny boy got "tee tee" just like you," Baby Black says.

"What the hell you say, girl?" Hinton asks.

"Dig, bro, some of these chicks got dicks—you know, he/she's. But Lil Black here is going to hook you up with some pure-D, P.I. pussy— just reach up in they drawers to make sure," Johnson laughs.

Baby Black waves to three girls, all fine. Two with permed-out Afros, and one with long, straight Asia-girl hair. "This Brother Hinton, he take one of you tonight. Now show him you little girls so he know you not Benny boy."

All three unzip their double knits, pull down their drawers, and reveal to Lewis three almost-hairless P.I. snatches.

"Goddam, Johnson, this place is boss. I want all three," Hinton crows.

"Easy, greasy, it's a long slide. Just one at a time. Take Susu here, she's got the biggest tits in the hooch. You're gonna have big fun tonight."

"Right on, Johnny, big-time Teddy Hinton is on the scene."

Meanwhile, Starchild and her sailor are snuggled up at the table, and he's buying another twenty-peso ladies' drink. "Baby, you're the finest lady in this joint. Let's split and get a room right now," The second-class gunner's mate on his first West Pac is pleading.

"Not tonight, fleet sailor. I got a customer who pay already, but tomorrow I be free just for you," Starchild says while rubbing the sailor's crotch with a small foot, while the band goes into the *Ohio Players hit, "I Want To Be Free."*

Across Rizal Street at the New Jolo Club, the freak show is at full tilt. Girls are using their vaginas to smoke cigarettes, pick up peso coins, and shoot ping-pong balls into baskets, all to the incredulous hoots and hollers of a packed house of wasted fleet sailors.

At Papa Joe's *Dexter Gordon's "Go"* is playing on Joe's system, and we're talking about America and life in general. The thing about the Green Dolphin for me is not just the music and the fact that Joe always has real US package-store liquor and makes ice from distilled water—all of which make this the best drinker's bar in Olongapo—but it's Papa Joe Pettaway, the teacher, philosopher, and man who makes this the best club in the world, bar none.

"You know, Juney, the idea of America is like heroin to the rest of the world: life, liberty, and the pursuit of money, fast cars, and blond pussy got the whole world on a jones. But on the real side, it's just another bullshit scam set up by a bunch of rich ofays to keep themselves rich, using guilt and fear of the black man to keep the system working while they rape, pillage, and kill worldwide. Not for me, Juney. I ain't dying a hypocrite in the land of lies."

"I dig you, Pops, but things are changing back home. Brothers are getting some breaks, and the young whites got open minds. These little kids being born today, black and white, won't have all this bull jive to cut through. They gonna be a better generation."

"Yeah, son, it might be better, but the fat-cat ofays that run America will always rip off the people, black and white. As long as you got the black at the bottom, these other fools can't see that they're being played too. I hope you get your new world, son, but get all you can for you and yours, while you can. And remember, although you were born in America, you'll never be treated as good as any white man fresh off the boat from Russia, Germany, or anywhere else. If you can get down with that, more power to you, but it's not my bag. Never again," Joe says.

Dexter was wailing, and I sipped my Jack while mulling over Papa Joe's words, wondering if race was the reason Goins' body had washed up in the Shit River. Old Denny B stopped by Club Viking a couple of times; aside from the usual racist babble, he didn't hear or see anything that would suggest a murder ring.

The Connie stayed in port for eight days and aside from the usual drunk-and-disorderly conduct, nothing of note happened with the battle-group sailors. There was an incident involving a stationdito[19], who upon learning he made chief petty officer, was partying hard at Marylyn's Number One Bar in the barrio and decided to take a swan dive into the river. Unfortunately, where he landed was only three feet deep. He broke his neck and ended his Navy career. Never got to put those khakis on. Starchild saw her guy, Doug, with one of Baby

---

[19] Stationdito – Military personnel stationed in Subic

Black's girls, and the shit-eating grin he wore told Starchild that Doug had found his P.I. hooker. Renda lost Dawson at the High Plains that first night and had to cover for him when their duty section rolled around. Dawson picked up a fine bikini dancer, she flipped for him and moved him into her crib. Now he's in love. No shit. It was an uneventful port call for old *CV64*, now they were off to Singapore and Karachi, and wouldn't return to P.I. for at least two months.

Things were slow, very few ships were in port: the old diesel sub Greyback, and the repair ship the USS Jason, which stays tied up for so long it's known as building number eight, and for five days the 7th Fleet Command Ship, Okie City. All the Stationditos from Subic and Cubi, the various marine units at the five-hundred-man camp, and the VP boys—nothing to get Olongapo geeked up like a carrier port call.

At HQ that morning Tyler even remarked what an uneventful liberty the Connie had. "Maybe these new volunteers are too high-tone to really raise some hell."

"Just give 'em time, Skip," Denny said, adding, "Once they realize they ain't got no war, a pocket full of cash and more tail than the

Chinese Red Army could fuck, it's bohica, baby."

"Okay, Denny, you and Ricky give me an update on Goins, and your take on the security situation with Roberto's boys."

Denny and I followed Tyler into his office and updated him on the deal with Roberto, including the pipe he'd found. Tyler let us know that the fraud division was going to take the lead on this one, and that it was being played off as a burglary ring, run by some P.I. nationals who worked at Cubi, and the dudes who got popped were a couple of the ringleaders. This tactic seemed to get Mayor Horton and the newspaper boys off the Navy's case.

"Skip, I've been trying to track down Goins' old lady. Her name's Monique, but this broad is hard to run down from here in P.I. Maybe we should have some stateside boys snoop her out," I say to Tyler.

"We might have to, Rick, but what were you able to turn up?" Tyler asks.

"Well, seems like Goins had changed his allotment and was sending it to his mom up in Cleveland. Grandma has their two kids, but

Monique took a powder."

"You spoke to Grandma?"

"I did, Skip. Called her from the MARS station. She was still pretty upset about her son's death, but she said when Monique dropped off their kids with her, she gave her three grand—cash—and said Goins had run off with 'Suzy Wong.' That was about six weeks ago. She hasn't seen or heard from her since. In any case, I let Grandma know to have Monique contact us if she were to hear from her."

"Okay, Ricky, I guess we've got to wait that angle out. What about the racial angle, Denny?"

"I don't know, Tyler. But I doubt these Viking boys were behind it. I got these knuckleheads pegged as poseurs and wannabe outlaws. Their belief is that the white man is superior to all other people, and the blacks and others are sub humans who should do the menial and dirty work of the master race."

"Okay Denny, that's just the typical claptrap that these clowns spout. Relate it to Goins' murder."

"That's just it, Tyler. These shit-for-brains feel the best place for the black man is overseas fighting the white man's wars. I can't peg them knocking off Goins for that reason alone," Denny says.

"All right, gents, let's try to get a hand on this thing PDQ. There's a lot of political pressure being laid on by a black congressman on behalf of Goins' family, and the brass wants this thing wrapped up. I don't need to tell you that Subic Bay is a powder keg, and if this turns out to be a racial murder, it could be the spark that sets it off. All right, gents, shove off and carry on."

As we leave Tyler's office, I eyeball Denny and say, "What's this subhuman shit?"

"Look, Ricky, I was just quoting our redneck shipmates."

"Well, all you MFs can kiss my black ass," and Denny and I crack up as the other agents and office workers look at us and roll their eyes.

I was finally contacted via letter by a woman claiming to be Monique Goins. She had her facts right, knew both Goins' serial and Social Security numbers. And the SSN she gave for herself matched what was in Goins' file. The letter was postmarked Las Vegas, which meant she could be anywhere. I contacted the local Vegas PD and our MIS boys in Fallon, Nevada, on the off chance that she hung around.

As for their time together, Monique said they'd met at Wilberforce University in Ohio as freshmen in 1962, but Goins quit school in 1964 because of family matters and joined the Navy. Monique finished school, and they married in 1966. By 1970 they'd had two daughters, and Goins was well on his way to becoming an aviation electrician, first class. Things had been going well for Goins. By 1975, he was being courted by two big civilian outfits, while at the same time, the Navy was grooming him as a limited-duty officer. Monique had started on a career of her own as a grade-school teacher, but when Goins got the six-month TAD orders to P.I., shit started going south. Goins' letters to Monique and his girls became infrequent. He managed to call only once, and then he Dear Johned her, told her by letter that he was in love with a woman he'd met in P.I. named Layla. Monique said she freaked out. Her and the girls' lives were built around Phil. She felt overwhelmed and lost. But then she started receiving envelopes with five grand US inside. Four of these envelopes came in October of 1975. Monique knew something wasn't right, but money talks, so she kept her trap shut and made arrangements to meet Phil at Norton AFB in San Bernardino, so he could tell her face-to-face what the real deal was. They were set to meet on January 5, 1976, but of course, Phillip Goins was dead as a doornail by then. When word that Goins had been offed reached Monique, she cracked. With the Dear John letter and twenty grand cash, she could smell a fat rat. She packed up the kids and split from Miramar for Cleveland, where she dropped off the kids and some cash with Goins' mom, then went on the lam. She also enclosed a picture from 1972 of a smiling AEI in dress blues, with a pretty wife and two little girls with bright eyes and beaming smiles—a happy little family. What a drag this case is, I thought.

I had to requalify with handguns on May 1st, and this reminded me that it had been four months since Phillip Goins' corpse had washed up on the banks of Shit River, just like any other piece of refuse, but this man was not garbage. He was a husband, a father, and a GI, and I'd made up my mind to find out how he ended up dead in the water in Olongapo City.

I took Nea to the movies later that day to see Sonny Chiba's *Bodyguard,* and Charles

Bronson's *Stone Killers*. Chiba and Bronson were my favorite actors. To me they always carried themselves like they knew what time it was—not like most of the cupcake-assed Hollywood actors. The theater was old and dilapidated, and if you dropped some popcorn, you could hear the rats munching down, but the flicks were great. The audience was just like black folks back home, cheering and talking to the screen, we had a great time. After the flicks we ate Mexican food at Papagayos. Nea whispered in my ear, asking if I was ready for her Filipina taco. I told her to get the hot sauce ready.

We ended the night at the Foxy Brown. The P.I., of course, had a heavy Spanish tinge to it, the new disco music lent itself to the cha-cha, mambo, salsa, and other Latin dances. My mom had taught this style of dancing to my brother, Rey, and me when we were kids. Nea had also been a dancer from a young age. We were tearing the dance floor up, and the other dancers gave us space to do our thing. When the band slowed it up with some *Delfonics,* Nea and I melted into each other on the dance floor. I never felt those fireworks of being in love with Nea, but I was more comfortable with her than with any woman I'd known.

"Many guys have come to you with a line that wasn't true and you passed them by......"

CHAPTER 7

My mom was a mixture of African, Caribe, Indian, and Spanish. She was short, with a face like a brown Audrey Hepburn and an athletic build. She was a great dancer and handball player. She passed away in 1957 when I was twelve years old. She'd worked as a nurse's aide at City of Angels Hospital on Temple Street in LA, and her life revolved around me, my big brother Reynaldo, our Pops Aaron, and her work at the hospital.

Mom's name was Rosalita, but everyone called her Rose. I took several traits from my mom— my brown complexion, thick, straight hair, and ambidextrous athletic ability, but our personalities were very different. My brother Rey was outgoing and friendly like my Mom, whereas I was quieter and more introspective, like my pops. It was my ability to use either my right or left hand that made firing pistols with either, fairly easy for me. It also gave me a great advantage in any type of hand-to-hand fighting.

After mom died so suddenly of a brain aneurysm at thirty-eight, Rey was drafted into the army, and Pops, who was a merchant marine, lost himself in work and some hard drinking. I was sent to live with my Pop's older sister Mabel, and her husband Fred. They lived on Western and Thirtieth Street in a two-story house with a yard about a mile and a half from the small four-room bungalow I'd grown up in on Thirty-Eighth and Budlong, not far from the Coliseum. My aunt and uncle were quite a bit older than my folks and had lived in LA since the early 1920s. They were staunch Baptists with four grown kids, but they loved me like a son and instilled in me their "You-can-make-it-if-you-try" attitude.

I was a fair student at Manual Arts High School, but an outstanding athlete—All-City in football as a defensive back, and in track in the 440. I hung out some, drank a little wine, smoked a little reefer, chased some skirt, and got into the Jazz scene a bit. My girlfriend in junior and senior year was Chantal Moore. A straight A student and a member of the marching band, who would eventually go to UCLA and become a lawyer. It was because of Chantal that I kept my nose clean.

Rey ended up in the Army Signal Corps and eventually went to work for RCA in Camden, New Jersey. He married and had three kids. Pop got involved with union work and remarried in 1962. By 1965 I had two younger sisters who called me Uncle Ricky. Since I went into the service, Dad and I have become more like brothers than father and son. I've had some rough breaks, but I also had teachers like Papa Joe and my aunt and uncle to encourage me. I'd always dreamed of being known as a man of honor who was skilled at his craft. The Navy gave me that craft. It was only my red-hot temper that at times derailed me. As I've gotten older, I've learned to keep it in check 98 percent of the time. But that last 2 percent is still pure-D hell.

I made it to the range and requalified, using my .38, which I'd used throughout my MIS career. I did so easily, both right- and left-handed, got my papers, signed off, and headed up to Cubi Point. I think because I'm ambidextrous, I approach problems by looking at both sides of a situation. Like this Goins case: on the one hand, what was Goins doing to get himself offed; and on the other, who or what benefited from his death? I wanted to sit in the quiet of the base library and try to sort out my thoughts. When I walked into the library, I was one of about eight people in the building, including the three librarians. I found a small table and chair in a corner and sat down to do some thinking.

Papa Joe's indictment of America was still ringing in my mind. All he said I felt to be true. The deck was stacked to keep the rich whites rich, and everyone else fighting for scraps and in debt—with the black man being excluded from the benefits of society and blamed for the ills that the crooked system produced. Joe wasn't a bigot, but he called America like he'd lived it, and he saw no place of dignity and respect for a black man back in the States. I felt more hope for my country. I'd seen a lot of change just since 1963 when I enlisted. Attitudes—both black and white—were evolving. I felt this new generation of kids that were the ages of my sisters, ten and twelve, would be the ones who could live out America's creed of equality and justice.

Papa Joe's buddy, R.L. Rossell, was my navy mentor and had a completely different view of the Country that he and Joe had served through two wars. R.L. believed there was opportunity for anyone regardless of where they were from or what color their skin was. It just meant hard work, and as he used to say, "stick-to-itiveness." He and his wife proved it in their lives. After retiring from the Navy, R.L. went home to South Carolina and became a contractor, building the same-style suburban ranch houses that had sprung up all over the North for black professionals in the South. His wife, Mary, became one of the first black female assistant principals in the newly integrated school system. R.L. felt he'd paid his dues in full, was entitled to first-class citizenship, and was willing to fight to be accorded those rights.

Both Joe and R.L. had grown up fatherless in the South during the twenties and thirties. They both suffered the slings of racism and poverty. Both served America honorably during the wars, but their views of their birth land were 180 degrees apart. I admired and respected both men, but I was more of a glass-half-full guy like R.L. Having a Dominican mother and a redbone father made me appear racially nondescript. Most American blacks or whites considered me to be Cuban or Puerto Rican—sometimes even East Indian or Arab—but rarely African American. This gave me more mobility than most blacks when dealing with whites. They just didn't know where to pigeonhole me. I often felt myself on the outside looking in at the whole psychotic racial scene in the US. Maybe that was the reason I loved the gridiron so much as a youngster; it was the first level playing field I was able to participate on. Once I put on those pads and that helmet, my skin color, height, or any other physical characteristics were secondary to my skill level. If I could juke, run over, or knock a dude down, it was straight-up fair. The best man would win.

The military was one of the first institutions outside of sports to try integration. Although there was still much discrimination and bigotry, it was by far the most egalitarian segment of America. Both sport and service proved to me, beyond a doubt, that different races could live and work together with mutual respect. It will be a long time before brothers are on Wall Street, in Hollywood, or in the Ivy League. When the rich white men start a war, it's the poor boys of all colors who do the fighting.

I know I'll go back to America—the world—the place of my birth. I feel it can and will be better for my kids and grandkids. The words of James Brown start running through my brain:

"I don't want nobody to give me nothing; open up the door, I'll get it myself."

CHAPTER 8

I went by HQ, and our lead agent Tyler, told me he needed me to chopper up to the American Embassy in Manila and brief some assistant deputy under the ambassador on the Goins case. The chopper was to depart from Radford Field in Cubi at 0700 hours the following day. I stopped at the fleet reserve club and had a bowl of chili and a couple of San Miguel's, I'd decided to spend the night on base and crash early. Nea was used to me not showing up for days at a time due to my work. If she needed to get word to me, she could reach me through Rory. Since she was the widow of a GI, Rory had permanent dependent status, and thus could come and go on base as she pleased.

Early the next morning, I was on the flight line at Cubi Point, watching USMC Captain O'Brien's crew preflight the CH-46 Sea Knight twin rotor helicopter that would carry me and about ten others to Manila. When I arrived, I was to brief a cat named Hampton Morris.

"Hey, hey Peter Gunn what it is?" Captain O'Brien says, grinning.

"I'm just hitching a ride to Manila with you fine marine airdales because these P.I. roads are too fucked-up to drive."

"Ricky, my man, it's our pleasure. We'll have you in Manila most ricky tick."

"Right on, Captain. I know I'm cool when I leave the flying to you."

The preflight was finished. O'Brien and his copilot were in the cockpit. The other passengers and I enter the bird from the rear. The plane captain hands us all earplugs. There are two long benches, port and starboard on the 46. I belt myself in port side, near the aft, and put my plugs in. The smell inside the chopper is vaguely metallic, and when O'Brien cranks the twin rotors, the 46 makes a *whup, whup, whup* noise and shakes like an agitating washing machine. This motion usually has me ready to nod out, but I got such a good sleep the night before that I remain awake and alert. Once airborne, we leave Cubi and the beautiful hilly land around Zambales province, heading toward Manila and the embassy. After leaving the Olongapo area, we fly over miles of rice paddies. You can see the little nipa huts and caribou, P.I. versions of Texas longhorns. Everything seems at one and peaceful from five thousand feet, but on the ground it's hand-to-mouth poverty: if it doesn't rain, the farmers don't eat. It's hard for a Mickey-D greezin' American to dig that. Manila is a huge city, home to millions, with some of the most squalid slums in the world, and some superfine luxurious areas for the elites of the Marco's regime and foreigners. We chopper over this city, which stretches for many miles, and touch down at the US Embassy, which has its own helipad.

I walk in the diplomatic entrance, my badge getting me past the marine guard, state my business and present my ID at the front desk. I'm sent to an office on the second floor, room 282, which has a good-size outer office occupied by an attractive middle-aged Filipina. The nameplate on her desk reads "Linda Reyes." She's typing away on an IBM Selectric at what has to be eighty to a hundred words per minute. As I close the door, Linda looks up and says;

"Mr. Baptiste from MIS, Mr. Morris is expecting you. Have a seat, he should be with you soon."

"Thank you, Miss Reyes—and my name is Ricardo, Ricardo Baptiste," I say.

"Okay, Ricardo, and I'm Mrs. Reyes, but you may call me Linda."

I take a seat and pick up a copy of *Stars and Stripes* and go straight to the sports pages to check on my Dodgers. Looks like the month of May was starting out on a good foot. They were on a nine-game winning streak and just swept the Cardinals in four games. It looks like their infield of Garvey, Cey, Russell, and Lopes could be classic. After scanning the paper for a few minutes, Linda's intercom buzzes, and a voice says, "Show Mr. Baptiste in, please."

Linda stands up and walks around her desk, revealing some world-class legs. "Right this way, Ricardo," she says, showing me to a door on the other side of her room. As Linda opens the door, she introduces me, "Mr. Morris, this is Agent Ricardo Baptiste." She then motions me in to his office. The office has a window with a nice view. The furniture is Philippine narra wood. Morris sits at a large desk with a US flag and pictures of Ford, Rockefeller, and Kissinger, along with a diploma from Yale on the wall, and various family pictures on a credenza. As I walk to his desk, he stands, extending his hand.

"Hampton Morris. Pleased to make your acquaintance, Mr. Baptiste."

"Likewise," I say.

His hands are soft, but he has a firm grip. He is average height, a couple of inches shorter than I am—about five foot eight or nine—slim, balding, maybe in his early forties. Nothing remarkable, just an average white dude.

"Baptiste, glad you could make it. I'm liaison to the Philippine government for military affairs, and I need to be briefed on this alleged murder in Olongapo City."

I ponder him a moment before replying. He has that rich-dude, Chatsworth Osborne, Jr.'s, voice, but I figure that just goes with the Yale sheepskin. "Well, sir, from the angle of that .22 shot to the vic's skull, it doesn't appear to be a suicide."

"Yes, well, then, given that this was a murder, there are two angles that seem to stick out. The first being the drugs found on the body, the other being the possibility of a racially motivated attack."

"On the second point, we do not believe that this was perpetrated by racist elements within the US forces. Drugs, however, could be the real motive for Goins' death. The heroin that was found in his body cavity was an extremely high quality, pure grade—most likely from

Thailand or Burma. It appears that he was involved with some type of smuggling operation. That being the case, he could have been bumped off by any number of criminal elements, US or Filipino," I say.

"What do you feel in your gut, Baptiste? You've been on this case for a few months now. I have to admit we're getting a lot of pressure from Goins' mother, and she has a black congressman from Ohio demanding some answers—PDQ—if you follow my drift."

"Well, Mr. Morris, Goins had only been in P.I. six months or so. He was working on training some airdales at VRC45 on the *EA6B* aircraft. Within a few months, his wife started receiving large amounts of cash through the mail. After the cash started flowing, Goins Dear Johned the wife."

"Go on, Baptiste, you have the floor. I'm all ears."

"Goins was working closely with two civilian tech reps, a Jack McMillan and a Mike Zimmerman, both out of Long Island. He seemed particularly close to Zimmerman. They had rooms at the Hotel Royal, and both men were seen in the company of very tall, beautiful

Asian women. I've contacted and received statements from both McMillan and Zimmerman, and both were back in CONUS by early December, well before Goins was popped."

"Okay, Baptiste, can you wrap this up for me?"

"Well, Zimmerman said that Goins had flipped for this Asian fashion model and was trying to get her back stateside, which is why he took his thirty-day leave in PO Town. The easy explanation would be that this chippie was using Goins as a go-between to facilitate a dope-smuggling deal, and either he got greedy or turned chickenshit and got himself capped. Now, the woman might be dead as a doornail also, but I think she just played Goins, and when he was of no more use to her and her people—bing, bang, boom—they put his soul on ice."

"That's the long and the short of it. Goins was mixed up with a P.I. dope ring and was killed when he became a liability to their operation," Morris says.

"No, that's the short of it. I feel there's a lot more to this picture, and until I can locate that big gal, everything is going to stay fuzzy. I think the dope angle is plausible, but it's too pat. I believe this murder goes much deeper than dope."

"Ricardo, you're a sharp young fellow, and the scenario you laid out is very logical. As to what the bigger picture is, that could be a needle in a haystack, like who really shot JFK. I feel your drug explanation is very likely, but I'll give you a couple of weeks to locate that Asian model and show me another angle. After that, I'll need a full report from your station," Morris says.

He went on to remark on my appearance, "You know, Ricardo, I thought you would be an American Negro. I should have guessed from your name you were Cuban or Puerto Rican."

"My mother was from the Dominican Republic, but my dad was from South Carolina. I'm LA born and bred, as black American as cornbread and collard greens."

"I didn't mean anything derogatory; you just don't look Negro or black. You could be East Indian, Arab, or anything. Maybe you should consider the State Department. A fellow like you could be a real asset," Morris says.

"Thank you, sir, but I'm not Ivy League, and I like the job I'm in."

"Very well, young man, thank you for your time. Take my card. Feel free to contact me concerning this case or the Foreign Service. I hope to see that report soon." With that, Morris stands, and we shake hands again. He buzzes Linda and says, "Show Mr. Baptiste around the embassy. Maybe he wants to pick up some gifts."

Linda appears at the door to escort me to the embassy package store, where I pick up a bottle of Stoli for Papa Joe and some Makers Mark for myself. As we're leaving, I'm walking slightly behind Linda, digging her gorgeous gams, and a tall guy with a long ponytail, wearing hippie garb right out of the Haight, 1967, is walking towards us. He winks at Linda and says in perfect Manila Tagalog, "Como estaka, Mugunda?"

"Mebutti, Rudy," Linda giggles in reply.

After he passes, I ask Linda who he was. She says the name is Rudy Franco, and he used to be with the Peace Corps, but is now with USAID. I ask if there's a phone I can use to call back to my HQ. She escorts me to a secure phone and then heads back to her office. As I watch those fine legs twitch away, I think Mr. Reyes is one lucky SOB.

I get Tyler on the line. "Hey Skip...., this Ricky, I briefed Morris to his satisfaction. He's sold on the dope angle, but I think I convinced him there might be more to the story. Anyway, he said he's giving me a couple more weeks to try to fill in the blanks."

"Okay, Ricky. We can talk details when you get back."

"Look here, Skip, what's the chance of my pulling a forty-eight up here? I could use a little R&R, and Rolfie from Yokosuka's got a boss joint on Mabini Street."

"Okay, Ricky, you got your forty-eight, but you and Denny got to turn two when you get back."

"I appreciate it, Skip. My nose is already next to the grindstone."

"Carry on, young man," Tyler says and hangs up.

I leave the Embassy to hail a cab and I start thinking that Morris wants to get this shit off his plate ASAP, and a dope murder of a black GI fits the bill—no racial angle, just good old pure D greed. I believe it's much more, and I hope I can find something to back up my hunch. I also keep thinking about that dude, Franco. He seems vaguely familiar to me, but

116

I've never seen him before today.

CHAPTER 9

I get a cab right outside the embassy compound. Manila's streets, like many other Asian megacities—Hong Kong, Tokyo, Bangkok—are some of the most crowded and unpredictable in the world, especially for an American. I tell the cabbie to take me to the Pension Filipina, which is across town near the infamous Mabini Street, known far and wide as having a world-class red-light district. This is the street that Rolfie's Daktari Club is on.

Most American military officers or civilians in my pay grade would stay at one of the luxury joints like the Oriental or the Manila. For the price of a night in one of those cribs, I can spend a week at the Pension. The Pension is a glorified youth hostel that offers single rooms. A few years back it was profiled in some European travel magazines and has since become a way station for the young and hip from the US and Europe. It has a piano bar and lounge with good singers and combos that play light jazz and pop sounds. It takes a while to get across town in the midday Manila traffic; it seems as if every other car is a taxi, and there are countless Jeepneys—along with many tricycles, rickshaws, and pedestrians.

If Olongapo was mind-blowing, Manila was an explosion; the noise, color, and frenetic pace were crazy, and so was the stench and squalor of the streets. It was hard to believe that just outside the US Embassy, which could be a country club in LA, you're in stone Slumsville in short order.

When I arrive at the Pension, I see my old friend Eddie Resurrection at the front desk. Eddie and his wife, Rita, have managed the Pension for years and have known me for over ten, since I was a young sailor on the Coral Sea.

Eddie greets me warmly. "Ricky, my son, it's been a long time. Are you in Manila for business or fun?"

"Eddie, I guess it's some of both. But I've only got forty-eight; you got anything available?" I ask.

"Three-eighteen, your usual room, is open, and Maria is singing here this season, fresh from Macao. Her set starts at 7:00 p.m."

"Right on. I'd love to see her again," I say.

I give Eddie forty US dollars, which is about twice the going room rate for two days, grab my ditty bag, and head upstairs to room 318. I figure I'll catch a catnap and check Maria's show out before heading to the Daktari.

I'd crashed for a couple of hours before I'm awakened by a knock on the door at about 1745. I answer the door in my skivvies, which is how I'd nodded out. I see the oval-faced, long-haired, four-foot-eleven Maria Aguilar, who at thirty-eight still looks like a college girl.

"Hello, pogi. Still my bronze god," she says, and plants a lascivious kiss on my chest. I bend down and we kiss on the mouth, long and deep. She's wearing bell-bottom jeans and a peasant shirt. Maybe she's a hundred pounds soaking wet.

"Damn, doll. Don't you ever age? I feel like a cradle robber when I'm with you."

"Ricky, you know I could be your big sister," she says, laughing. "Eddie told me you were here, but I had to see you myself. You still make me see stars, honey."

"Well, baby, the feeling's mutual. So, what's going on?"

"I'm playing two sets a night during August— one from 7:00 to 9:00 p.m.—then 10:00 p.m. to closing. My playing is much stronger now. I toured with *Wattenabe* and some other Japanese musicians in Macao and Australia.

I'm learning to use space like *Miles* and *Ahmad Jamal*. You'll see tonight," she says excitedly.

This love of music, Jazz in particular, is one of many passions we share. "Hey, doll, you got me in moody's mood, dig?"

"Ricky, I've got to get ready for my set, but I'll see you in the bar, okay?"

"Yeah, okay, but I've got to go by a buddy's joint and check out a couple of things."

"My brother, Carlos is back from California. He's a real student activist now. You two should talk," she says as she kisses me again and grabs my Johnson and gently strokes me. "I'll take care of you and your friend here later," she says as she walks out the door.

Damn, that Maria's got my nose wide open. I'd been planning on having Rolfie hook me up with one of his certified freaks, but I got Maria on my mind now.

I shit, shower, and shave, and head downstairs to the piano bar. Rita is tending the bar, and on seeing me, pours me a double Jack on the rocks.

"Same, same, Ricky," Rita laughs.

"And you know that, Mamasan," I reply.

The room is big enough for about thirty people, but only eight are there at this early hour. Maria's set doesn't start for another half hour. There's a group of European tourists drinking Tiger and Heineken beers, speaking German or possibly Dutch; a couple of middle-aged Filipinos of the intellectual class; and a young Filipino with long hair, wire-rimmed glasses, and a goatee. The young guy waves me to his table, and when I get a closer look, I recognize him as Carlos, Maria's kid brother. I've known him since he was around twelve or thirteen, he looked up to me as a big brother. Carlos had always been smart, curious, and thoughtful. Maria sent him to San Jose State to become an engineer. He doesn't look like no engineer, he looks more like a young Che Guevara.

"Ricky, what it is, bro?" Carlos asks.

"Carlito, man, I hardly recognized you. What's good with you? What did you learn in the mighty world?" I sit down with my Jack and offer Carlos a Kool, which he accepts. I take one myself and fire them both up with my Zippo.

"You know, Ricky, I always knew America was rich and big, but I didn't realize how rich and how big until I got there."

"Yeah. It's the land of plenty," I say.

"Plenty of America got its wealth by exploiting the rest of the world; like here in P.I., putting in puppet regimes while ripping off other people's land and treasure and keeping them in poverty," Carlos says.

"Hold on, man, there's plenty of greed to go around. There's always a Shah or a Marcos willing to sell out their own for that mighty dollar bill," I say.

Carlos looks me dead in the eye and says, "Ricky, how can you justify that system? I've seen how blacks are treated in America—like dogs, without the rights or respect that a white man fresh off a refugee boat gets. I met black revolutionaries in Oakland, and all over, who know that the current system must be brought down. But that's your fight, Ricky. I just want the US out of P.I.," Carlos says.

"I dig where your head's at, but revolution by a distinctly visible armed minority in America is sure suicide. In America you have to have a revolution of the mind. People's eyes have to be opened, and attitudes changed. I didn't dig all of Dr. King's ways, but he was able to change minds, black and white, and that changed the country," I say.

"But, Ricky, more change is needed, and power yields to nothing but greater power."

I say, "The greatest power is the moral power of the truth, that's what King had. I've seen committed revolutionaries—men, women, and children—who were willing to live in tunnels, exist on small packets of rice, and fight to the death. Ain't no fat-assed American—black, white, or Puerto Rican—gonna give that kind of commitment for years at a time. Carlos, this is your country, you have numbers on your side.

"The Moros and Huks have been fighting for years, but it's the young and educated, like you, who have to teach and mobilize the masses. Maybe if enough people's minds are opened, you might achieve that goal," I say, surprising myself with my analysis, because I'd never put my thoughts concerning revolution into words before.

"Ricky, your insight is heavy. It's you who made me want to see America for myself. I learned much and am committed to changing my homeland."

Maria and her group enter at that moment. Maria is in an elegant black gown with a slit to her upper thigh. Her hair is pulled back with flowers in it, like Lady Day. She sits at the piano and plays the opening of *Ahmad Jamal's* tune *"Wave,"* as the bass and drums fall in on cue. Maria's playing is more dynamic and rhythmic than I'd remembered.

"Carlito, your big sis is pure TNT—brains, talent, and beauty," I say.

"Yeah, man, and she's still waiting for you," Carlos murmurs.

"She can do a lot better than me. I'm just a kid to her." I fire up another Kool and sit back and dig the sounds.

The song ends, the crowd claps enthusiastically, and Maria pulls the mike up and says, "Thank you, music lovers. That was *Ahmad Jamal's 'Wave.'* I'm Maria Aguilar, and this is my trio, with Jose Castro on bass and Oscar Gomez on drums. I'd like to point out my baby brother, Carlos, who is just back from college in America, and an old friend, Ricardo Baptiste. They're over in that corner," she says, pointing us out.

She then launches into *"Do You Know the Way to San Jose."* Maria's voice is *Astrud Gilberto* light, but her command of English and phrasing is more dynamic. I finish my Jack, which was poured so liberally that I had nursed it for an hour. As I stand up, Carlos also stands and gives me a soul-brother handshake. As I make my way out of the bar, Maria winks and blows me a kiss.

I leave the Pension and walk back to Mabini Street. Rolfie's joint, the Daktari, is about half a mile away. The Daktari is a large place with a jungle motif of bamboo and straw, and several dance platforms where thirty or more go-go girls shake it at all times. Along with a boss DJ and fantastic light and sound systems, Rolfie has a gross of women working in his place in all states of undress; 144 whores, as he likes to say. These women mingle, serve drinks, and all are the pay-for-play type.

The walk from the Pension reminds me of how similar Manila is to Puerto Rico or the Dominican Republic in architecture. I figure it's because they were all, at one time, Spanish colonies and had similar tropical climates. I'm in in my everyday uniform of Cuban guayabera shirt and khakis, with leather Puma kicks. The shirt color might change, but the khakis and the kicks are constant. There's a slight breeze this night, but after a block or so, I have a sweat going in the humid evening air.

As I'm walking, I think about Carlos' revolution talk and how after World War II, the US had set up first Magsayay, and later Marcos as strongmen who kowtowed to the US for their own personal profit and strategic and material gain. I guess America is the new Britain: an imperial power masked behind the image of a benevolent democracy. It's weird the impression foreigners have when they visit America. All are overwhelmed with the size and wealth—the brown, black, and yellow ones immediately sense the racism and discrimination, and how it's at odds with the US public relations line of equality and democracy. But many white Europeans note this as well. Rolfie once told me he'd visited the States in 1962 and could eat, sleep, shop, and travel at will; and I, who was born and bred in America, had none of those rights. As he put it, "My white skin makes me more American than you, although our countries fought two wars against each other."

I hope Carlos and his generation can one day run their own country. These heavy thoughts are running through my head as I walk into the Daktari, *Osibesa's* blasting from the sound system. Rolfie plays youth music from around the world: *Fela, Bob Marley, Led Zeppelin, The Stones*—you name it—all at hyper volume. The girls are gorgeous and buck wild, and are from all over Asia: the Philippines, Thailand, Vietnam, China, Malaysia, and even some white women from Australia. Rolfie spots me from his perch behind the main bar and screams, "Ricardo Baptiste, the Latin soul brother!"

"You got that right, Rolfie-san. What it is, Herr Rommag?" I try to holler over the music.

"Ricardo let's go to my office. It's too damn loud out here."

"I can dig it, but it's your joint. Turn that shit down."

"No way, man! I don't want my customers thinking, I want them drinking and spending," Rolfie laughs.

We duck into a plush soundproof office in the rear of the club where Rolfie plays his music-organ trios. He's got *Jimmy Smith* and *Wes Montgomery* on a seven-inch reel, jamming *"Road Song."* Rolfie looks at me and grins.

"Ricardo, I've been trying to get you and KC up here for months. Now the Frogs show up yesterday and here you are, the knockoff squad returns."

"What do you mean, the Frogs? You sayin' they in Manila?"

"Manila? Hell, they're here in my club. They have a private room and a dozen international freaks upstairs. It will blow their minds to see you in here."

"Well, lead the way, maestro."

We leave Rolfie's office, climb a spiral staircase, and enter a cipher-locked door, into a purple velour room with dim lights and spinning mirrored balls. Among a dozen women, some nude and all wearing no more than a bikini, are Ty and Deke. Ty copped the 'Deadeye' moniker in Nam where he and Deke were an almost mythic sniper team. Their trademark kill was a shot through the left eye. This struck much fear through the NVA and VC and much awe among US troops, many of whom never knew this deadly duo was black. Ty and Deke had become UDT SEALs in the mid-sixties. Like ham and eggs, they were two completely different individuals who made a dynamite team. Ty, Deke, and Rolfie were all about ten years my senior. After the war and retirement from the Navy, the Frogs continued to ply their trade as mercs and, from the looks of things, business must have been good.

Ty looked over at me and broke out in a grin, saying, "Rick Lee, what you know good, baby boy? Long time - no see. Ty added the middle name of "Lee" to anyone he dug, so Ricardo Baptiste became "Rick Lee." To me, it was an honor to have that "Lee" added to my name, as Ty was one of the most highly regarded special-forces operatives of his time, the consummate professional. But his profession was death on demand. Hey, look here, Deke, Rolfie brought us sweet Peter Jeter," He said.

"Yeah, the woman's pet, the man's threat, and the punk's pinup. Guess we got to lock these bitches up before this wavy-haired trick baby pulls the baddest hammers," Deke snarls.

I look at these two who are now smiling damn near ear-to-ear, and say, "Fellas, I ain't about to cockblock stone killers like y'all. It's just you big, ugly splibs scare broads."

"Fuck you, ya pussy-licking spic. These bitches tell me how much dick they want, and I roll it out just like they ask. That's why they call me 'Deadeye Dick.' One shot from old Johnson here and they be hooked," Ty says.

At this, everyone in the room cracks up, including Ty. The Frogs stand up, and we dap and hug each other.

Deke calls out to Rolfie, "Hey, Rolfie. Bring them little-bitty bitches up here for Ricky."

"I don't need no bitches, little or big. I got a fine hammer back at my hooch. I just dropped in to check out Rolfie's action."

"Well, then, stick and stay and check out these little twins. They gonna pop your wig, bro," Ty says.

Rolfie splits, and Ty tells the women to dance, strip, or get drunk while we catch up. The music is *The Jazz Crusaders, "Southern Comfort,"* low and mellow. The women are walking around topless; a couple buck-naked are drinking, talking, and dancing around us, but giving us space to talk. It seems their work was taking them to South Africa and the Middle East. The cash they pulled in was crazy.

"You know when the war ended for us in '73, I was set like a fat rat in a cheese factory. My old lady got greedy and blew a hole through my ducats, so I went back to work. I called Deke in '74, and he said he was good to go. We been rolling ever since. Boy, you're looking at some black millionaires right here." Ty explained.

The Frogs are drinking ice-cold Russian standard vodka, neat in large tumblers. I light up a Kool and pour myself a liberal hook of communist oil. Man, that cold shit hits the spot. Rolfie returned with two of the most beautiful, well-built brown midgets, four feet tall each, that I'd ever seen.

"Gentlemen, the Malay twins for your viewing pleasure. These ladies bend 360 degrees but will not break anything but your bank account."

The two diminutive beauties stripped naked and proceeded to oil each other up; then with a two-headed dildo, they rode, humped, sucked, and filled every orifice of their bodies to the utter amazement of myself, the Frogs, and even Rolfie and the other women. I had a China girl rubbing my Johnson while playing with herself. Ty and Deke were smothered in tits and ass as the *Crusaders' - "A Ballad for Joe Louis"* played in the background. Mellow sounds for a wild scene. The twins' show went on for about thirty minutes, during which time my little China doll had walked me to a corner and jerked both me and her off. I guess Maria won't bust the easy nut tonight. When the twins' set ended, Rolfie hustled them out, saying some Jap businessmen were renting them for two thousand US for the rest of the night. The girl I was with cleaned me up and said, "You take me home tonight, soul bruddah."

"Not tonight, doll. I got other plans, but Deke and Ty will party like this for days. You gonna make plenty cash."

As I walk back to where the Frogs are sitting, there's a long-haired dude talking to them. I didn't see him come into the room, but I recognized him as the cat from the embassy.

"Fast Franco, you just missed the little-bitty twins, man. They a sho' nuff show," Ty says.

"Right on, Ty. I'll have to catch them. Who's your pal? I think I've seen him elsewhere today," Franco says.

"Oh, this here is Mr. Ricardo Baptiste, late of Cam Ranh Bay and other garden spots up north," Ty says.

"Saw you at the embassy today," I say.

"Yeah, okay. Linda tells me you're MIS out of Olongapo. I'm Rudy Franco, USAID," Franco says, extending his hand. We shake square-style.

"I heard Rolfie had some prime pussy in this joint and that's no BS, but I'm here to talk to Ty and Deke, and I can see that now isn't the time or place. Why don't we get together in a day or two, guys?" Franco says.

"Right on, Kimosabe, you call it," Deke says.

"Hey, Franco, have we met before? Maybe in PO Town or LA?" I ask.

"No, man, I'm strictly Manila, but I've heard there's some prime young tail in Olongapo," Franco says.

"Yeah, man, tenderloin groin."

"I'll look you up if I get over in that direction. Meanwhile, I need to see you two in the next forty-eight," Franco says, addressing the Frogs.

"Okay, boss, we heard you the first time. How about tomorrow in Rolfie's private office? Eleven hundred hours? That cool?" Ty asks.

"Okay, guys. See you then," Franco says as he leaves.

The music has changed to some *Quincy Jones*, *"Walking in Space,"* and the women are starting to show some of the effects of the vodka: laughing, stumbling on high heels, and pulling what's left of their clothes off. I'm not feeling much pain myself.

"Hey, Ty, who the hell is that dude?" I ask.

"That's a man who leads a life of danger," Ty says.

"I can dig it," I reply, and pour a short hook of the Russian vodka and take in this scene. Twelve drunk nude or near-nude beauties, two high-paid assassins, and me, a broke-ass MIS agent. Ain't this a bitch.

"Look here, fellas, it's been a stone gas, but I got to duff. How long y'all gonna be here?" I ask.

"Rick Lee, we're here for a while. Stop back by, baby bro. You always cool with us," Ty says.

I give Ty and Deke a soul handshake and split, shaking my head. I felt that I knew Franco from someplace.

When I get back downstairs, the main club is going full tilt. *Manu Dibango's "Soul Makossa"* is blasting. The girls are strutting and shaking, and the big shots from Tokyo and Yokohama are spending like drunken sailors. I find Rolfie and tell him I'll stop back by the next day. As I walk back out to Mabini Street, I realize my head is bad. Those damned Frogs got me juiced. I float through the nighttime Manila streets on my way back to the Pension, the thought crosses my mind that I've given Morris ample reason to write Goins off as a drug dealer. That being the case, I owe it to the Goins family to find out the truth and not have him written into eternity as a criminal, if he wasn't one. Even in my bent state of mind, this case is like a monkey on my back.

The walk back to the hotel clears my head a bit. It's close to one a.m. When I walk through the bar, Maria is on her last set. She looks at me with a lascivious smile, to which I lick my lips in reply. Maria then changes a verse in *"The Girl from Ipanema"* to *"tall and bronze and young and strong, the fella from LA city goes walking . . .,"* and I keep walking up to room 318.

Once inside I wash up, strip down, lock the door, and turn the fan on and nod out. I'm awakened by the sound of the door unlocking, opening, and then being closed and locked. Maria is in the room, the black gown is dropping from her shoulders revealing her aroused, naked body, which is full of lust and anticipation. The feeling is mutual.

CHAPTER 10

The dawn sunlight creeping between the Venetian blinds wakes me. Maria's small, taut body is curled under my arm, she is sound asleep. I've got a stone-piss hard-on, and my head feels like mush. I rarely get hangovers, but white booze leaves my head feeling spongy. I extricate myself from Maria, which is not hard to because she sleeps like a log and walk into the head and try to aim my stiff dick into the commode, then proceed to piss in three different directions. I wash up and crawl back into bed. Maria is still out like a light. Our lovemaking has always been nice and easy. We've been completely comfortable with each other from jump street. Maria is very passionate, but soft and tender. Not a rowdy screamer like Nea, for whom lovemaking is a fifteen-round title fight. Maria likes to climb on top and ride. Her eyes glazed and her breathing heavy, there's no hollering, scratching, or biting. Just a slow, smooth pleasure ride. I like it any which way I can get it. All women are unique for me. That's where Maria and I differ. Once my nose gets open, I'll ball almost any woman, and a lot of women I've met are horny MFs, just like me. But Maria is different. She doesn't give up any trim on impulse. She doles it out when and with whom she chooses, always on her terms. When we first got together, she claimed she had never enjoyed sex until she was with me. That blew my mind because she was a good deal older than I was. I started thinking, Damn! I'm a regular Casanova Brown. Lady killer of the first order. But as we got to know each other, I realized that she felt at ease with me, probably because of my youth. This allowed her to let her guard down and enjoy herself with me. She knew that I wouldn't judge or categorize her in any manner. I just dug her for being herself.

The sunlight is more prominent now and rushes through the blinds. The sounds of the streets are starting up. Maria awakens with a long, slow yawn and greets me with a smile of perfect teeth, a rare thing in the third world. She rolls over on her side and starts talking music.

"Ricky, did you hear how I'm using space in my playing, like *Miles* and *Jamal*. It makes my music more expressive of me."

"Yeah, Mary. I did dig that. You used to be all notes like *Liberace*, but your playing fits your singing now."

"I want my own sound, Ricky. As a jazz musician and singer, I want to create, not just imitate."

"That's cool, doll. But people pay to hear you do *Dionne* and *Astrud.*"

"One day I'll have my own signature songs like those ladies. You know Ricky, *Dionne's* coming to Manila this summer, but I might have a gig in Tokyo when she's here."

Maria then starts to lick my chest and massage my Johnson back to a raging state. She climbs back on me, and we make some early-morning love as the sun rises over Manila.

After showering, I get dressed and Maria went back to her room to change. We go downstairs for breakfast together; Eddie and Rita are looking at us with sheepish grins. It's always the same, anyone can spot lovebirds. We take our breakfast continental-style. After coffee and a smoke, we leave the Pension and kiss before going our separate ways. Maria is going to Quezon City to spend a couple days with her folks. By the time she returns, I'll be back in Subic. After I put Maria in a taxi, I hail one for myself and head to a gold dealer on Roxas Boulevard.

My night with Maria had been enjoyable on many levels: physical, emotional, and spiritual. But while she had waited for me with her passion rising, I, like a true whoremonger, was drinking and being serviced by a Chinese hooker. This was one of the reasons that, although I loved Maria and believed she also loved me, we would not make it as a couple. Aside from the age difference, there was her dedication to her music, and mine to my police work. Deep down, I knew my inability to be faithful to one woman was something Maria would never accept. I believed that many successful couples were so, less because of love, and more because of mutual respect and compatibility, which is what I have with Nea, and what Aunt Mabel and Uncle Fred seem to have.

During the cab ride I plan out my day, which consists of checking the gold market and then meeting with Rolfie, who's my buyer. For about a year now it's been legal for US citizens to buy gold, which seemed to be depressing the prices, which were around $125 US per ounce. Right now, the best price I got was $120 US per ounce through a Filipino with Israeli connections. I got into the gold-buying habit from hanging with Romeo. He always said, "Paper ain't shit, but gold is good anytime, anyplace."

After making my gold deal, I find a small bistro, sip an espresso, and smoke a Kool. I start to think of the dead sailor again. Goins was my age, in my old service, and had two little kids who deserved better than their daddy dying behind a dope deal. I feel in my gut that this dude had been bumped off for reasons other than dope or race. I feel he was the tip of a big scam that involved many folks of all stripes. I'm determined to find the real deal about his murder. After my coffee break, I hail another cab to Rolfie's joint. I had a good price and twelve hundred US that I would give Rolfie to make my buy. We'd watched each other's backs since my days in Yokosuka, him giving me intel from the street, and me trying to keep him out of harm's way. It's worked out well, we've both prospered. Much like Romeo, Rolfie and I are in the same game, but at times on different teams.

I arrive at Daktari at around 1400 hours. The club is still in stand-down mode. A few of the cleanup crew are swabbing the decks and resetting chairs and tables. There are some laid-back sounds on the system, and a handful of girls are there, along with Rolfie, Ty, and Deke. Big guys, each over six feet and more than 220 pounds, they make me—at five eleven, 200 pounds—feel like a sophomore at a seniors' party.

"Yo, Rick Lee, I know you was tight when you split, but did you TCB with your piano lady?" Ty asks.

"Man, you mother-humpers got way too much intel. You know we got righteously down, my brother," I say.

"Right on! Do it to death, Blackstone," Deke crows.

"Hey, Rolfie, get these commies some of that Soviet oil, and give a brother some Black Jack on the rocks," I say. As Rolfie sets us up, I pull a Kool from the bottom of my pack and light up.

Deke says, "Hey, homie, let me cop a square." I hand him the pack of Kool's.

This prompts Rolfie to ask, "Why do you soul brothers always take your cigs out backwards?"

"Because you never know where a motherfucker's mitt's been," I say.

"All right now, Ricky, school this chump," Deke says.

Rolfie laughs and says, "I heard that." He then puts on an album by *Charlie Earland* called *Intensity*. It features *Lee Morgan*, and it is indeed intense. "Ricky, I got this record in your honor," Rolfie says, handing me the album jacket. We knock back that round, and Ty orders up another and starts giving me his pitch about some independent contracting.

"Lookie here, Rick Lee, you talk spic, frog, gook, and half-assed English. You look Arab, Indian, Flip, whatever. Man, you can move around much of the world and not get a second look. The only place you get sniffed at is back in CONUS, and they don't know what the hell you are. Man, six months with me and Deke is three or four years of MIS pay, and there's no taxes—cash on the barrel head."

"Hey, I hear you, Ty, but I like this cop gig. Nobody is shooting at me on a regular basis, plenty of freedom, and lots of tail," I say.

"You a jive mickey ficky. With the dust we talkin', you can have all the freedom and tail you want, and much cash left over, dig?" Deke says.

143

"I can dig it, Deke. It just ain't my scene. I got my fill with you fools up north in Laos, Cambodia, or wherever we were at."

Ty smiles and says, "All right, baby boy. I'm just trying to pull your coattail, so you can get all the way out while you're still young. Hell, five years of this and you're set. What that make you, thirty-five, thirty-six? I know you can dig that, and I know you got schemes and dreams. Man, you gots to take some to make more."

"Yeah, fellas, but y'all scheme ain't my dream. I'm like Sinatra. I gotta do it my way."

"Right on, little brother. I guess we can't recruit every hood off the corner."

Ty, Rolfie, and I chuckle at Deke's comment. Rolfie flips the *Earland* LP and sets us up again. "Typhoon season is supposed to be bad this year," Rolfie says.

"Good. Wash some of this Southeast Asia shit away," says Ty.

We drink, laugh, talk about the twins and various other freaks we've known. They told me they had a gig in Central America that was tailor-made for me. I again declined the invite. By now it was close to 1800, and the club was open for business. I said adios to Ty and Deke and found Rolfie back in his office. I gave him twelve hundred US and the dealer's address for the gold. Along with the cash, I handed Rolfie a note detailing another inquiry I wanted him to make for me.

"I'll look into both matters, my friend, but you keep your powder dry," Rolfie says.

"I'll be back soon. Make sure those twins are still here. I'm bringing KC with me, and those little broads will blow his military mind."

Rolfie and I shake hands. I split, walking back the same Spanish-tinged streets, thinking I've been approached twice in two days for some spy-versus-spy shit. I start to wonder how long the puppet masters have had me on their radar. When I reach the Pension, there's a Filipino tenor player sitting in for Maria. He's not bad, but not up to the level of Maria's rhythm section. I decide to have a Mexican dinner at a joint called Barrio Fiesta. The food is good, it reminds me of being back home in LA. After dinner, I walk over to a little joint that caters to merchant sailors, called the Quayside. It's run by an Aussie and is a nice laid-back spot. No dancers or hostesses, just an older, quiet crowd. I have one Jack on ice and head back to the Pension. I've got an early flight back to Subic, and I have to debrief Tyler in the afternoon.

CHAPTER 11

Early the next day, I shit, shower, shave, and pack my overnight bag, then head to the kitchen for a cup of mud and some toast. Eddie makes his coffee thick and black, just like Navy issue, and I love it. I say my good-byes to Eddie—Rita's still sleeping—and assure him I'll be back soon. I walk to Mabini Street, hail a taxi, and head to the US Embassy for my 0800 flight. Once through embassy security, I make my way to the helipad. My name is on the manifest. Old Hampton Morris hooked me up. At 0745 a CH 46, this one manned by sailors, arrives. Some naval officers disembark, and the other civilians and I get on. We're told that this chopper has to make a pickup at Camp John Hay in Baguio City, up in the mountains of Luzon. A beautiful base with an eighteen-hole golf course. The climate is surprisingly cool, and the air is very fresh. This detour means we'll arrive at Cubi Point around 1100. After strapping in and putting on a set of Mickey Mouse's, the rhythmic rocking of the 46 has its usual sleepy effect on me. After checking out the crew of two Navy LTs and an E4 crew chief, my fellow commuters—two middle-aged white civilians—and I settle in for a little rest.

When I awaken, we're landing at John Hay and picking up some officers' wives who'd been on a shopping trip. They bought plenty of loot along with them. It took a four-man working party to load it all on and it took up most of the chopper. Once we're airborne again, I nod back out and don't wake up until we're touching down at Cubi Point. I thank the crew and head for the terminal to grab a taxi. "Top of the Mark," I say to the cabbie, and we head off for the CPO club in Cubi, it's almost time for the lunch rush. I order a San Miguel and some chili dogs. The ice-cold San Miguel washes off the chopper dust, and I reflect that a cold, frosty beer has got to be one of God's true pleasures. I phone HQ to speak to Tyler and let him know I'm back.

"Hey Skip, Ricky. I'm in Cubi. Thought I'd check on when we debrief," I say.

"Ricardo let's meet at 1600 hours."

"Aye aye, Skip."

I hang up, finish my brew, and order another. I feel that there's some shit in the wind. Skip never calls me "Ricardo" unless his jaws are tight about something. The club is starting to fill up with hungry, thirsty CPOs so I down my brew and split.

At 1534 hours I arrive back at HQ in Subic. I open my mail and other correspondence, there's a note from the photo lab letting me know the flicks of that pipe that Roberto's men found are ready for pick up. At 1600 on the dot, Denny saunters into HQ, looks me dead in the eye, and says, "DILIGAF."

"Do I look like I give a fuck? Is that all you've got to say, Denny?" I reply.

"Why the hell am I here for your debrief? They didn't see fit to send me on a Manila boondoggle. Now my liberty is being curtailed to hear your Charlie Sierra story," Denny continues.

About this time, Tyler shouts from his office, "Hey, Martin and Lewis, get your swinging cranks in here ASAP and cut the BS."

As we enter Tyler's office, he looks up from his desk and says, "Well, gents, it looks like Rick's brief went so well that I'm being told to wrap up this case ASAP. Rick, you write up the report with your conclusion of the murder, most likely drug related."

"What the fuck over Skip!?" I holler. "I told

Morris that was just one possible scenario, that this thing was much bigger. That dope shit don't even scratch the surface! My voice is rising now. "Morris said I had a couple more weeks, and you said for me and Denny to run this one all the way down to the nitty-gritty. Now, what gives? I ain't writing jack-shit until I know the story," I say.

Tyler looks me dead-on, his steel-gray eyes narrowed to slits, and in measured tones, he says, "I don't give a rat's ass which one of you bullshit artists writes it up, I want it on my desk by close of business tomorrow. Are we straight!? Ricardo, we're all ex-military, this here is the Military Investigative Service, and the brass that signs our paychecks says get this case off the books. Comprende?"

Now Denny throws in his two cents, "Look, Tyler, this case is more than dope and greed. This kid, Goins, was an AJ squared-away sailor with a wife and kids. Be a shame to tag him as a dope pusher."

"Look, gents, this is way beyond my pay grade. There's all kinds of pressure from a congressman back in Ohio. The brass and other agencies want this case gone. So, let me spell it out - This case is closed on our books tomorrow, period! We pass it up the chain," Tyler says.

I explode, "Goddammit, Skip! That's pure bullshit! This shit ain't near closed! It's loose ends! Let us try to tie them up. This is a big-time okey-doke here."

"Ricky, I understand your frustration, but it is what it is. Denny, you write up the report. Ricky, give Denny your notes. I don't want to hear any more on this matter. The man's dead; we can't bring him back. We just write up what we got and let the Navy decide how to rule his death."

Although he never raised his voice, the fact that his face flushed red and I could hear a trace of West Virginia in his voice let me know Tyler was royally pissed.

"Look, Skip, me and Ricky will wrap this up as per spec. I'll cool the Cisco Kid here down, and everything will be daijoubu."

"Right, Denny. You two do just that, and Ricardo, this is a job where we look at things from a cold, dispassionate viewpoint, no emotional involvement. I know Goins was a soul brother, but he was also a sailor like all three of us, and that makes him a shipmate. I don't like this any more than you two, but I intend that we do as ordered. Carry on, gents."

At that, Denny and I leave Tyler's office. I've got steam coming out of both ears. I'm mad as two motherfuckers.

Denny grabs my arm and says, "Look, pard, don't blow your lid. Like the song says, 'Don't let the sound of your own wheels drive you crazy.'"

"Denny, you know this is stone bullshit. It's a cover-up, man. This shit ain't nowhere close to right."

"Ricky, what the fuck you gonna do—start marching and sitting in? Half the shit you been in ain't right. Hell—Nam wasn't right. But it's over now. That squid Goins is dead, and we ain't bringing him back. We just press on. Let me buy you a Jack at Rory's. It's quiet there this time of day."

We head off base over Shit River Bridge in Denny's pickup. He parks in front of Rory's joint on Gordon Street. Inside the Nueva Filipina I sit at the bar nurse a triple Jack on ice, while Denny goes back to Rory's office. As I sip my Jack, I reflect on my Skipper Tyler and our friendship.

Jerry Lee Tyler was a career sailor. He joined in 1944 at seventeen and saw some action in the Pacific near the end of World War II. He was fresh from the coal mines and poverty of Appalachia. He said of himself that he was a "poor dumb hillbilly." While he may have been poor and from the hills, he wasn't dumb. By the time he retired in 1970, he was a Mustang LCDR with a master's degree in criminal justice, and he had been the CO of military police outfits in Da Nang, Yokosuka, and Seattle. He was tough—hard as nails, but fair. He was one of the best men I'd ever known. His wife, Sumiko, was from Yokohama and had come up rough as a war orphan. She was his match, pound for pound. They had two grown daughters who were married to servicemen. Tyler, like Denny, didn't have the cracker attitude that you'd expect from a West Virginia hillbilly. Having a Japanese wife and mixed-race kids gave him a different perspective on race. I knew Tyler to be a dude who judged on actions, not looks or words. It was cut-and-dried with Tyler: either you could do the job, or you were useless to him. He'd been a mentor to me since I'd worked with him in Yokosuka in 1969. This was his last station before he retired from active duty.

Yokosuka was jumping as an R&R stop for sailors and marines during Nam. It boasted a huge off-base EM club called the Sierra that had five bars, a movie theater, three restaurants, a package store, and a hotel—all under one roof. Of course, there were plenty pay-for-play girls. The operation was run by a short, stout dude from Jersey named Frankie Martinelli. He was a cool cat who took his cut right off the top. There were plenty of fights between squids from different ships, squids and Marines, and blacks and whites. Many of these were all-out brawls. One night I single-handedly broke up what was going to be a stone rumble. Some squids and grunts were going at it in the main bar area, chairs and fists were flying, girls were screaming, and shit was breaking. I arrived with several shore patrol, but the fracas escalated quickly when a sailor pulled a straight razor on a marine. I disarmed the sailor, dislocating his shoulder in the process, and in the same movement knocked the marine cold with a short right to the jaw. The GIs saw this, and all shit came to a halt. We restored order in the club and after that I became known as "Kato," the Bruce Lee character from the *Green Hornet*. Word of the fight got back to Tyler, and he started taking a personal interest in me and my career. I've been lucky in that I've had teachers and mentors throughout my life. They filled in for my pop and my brother, Rey, when we split up after Mom passed: my Aunt Mabel and her husband, Papa Joe, R.L., Tyler, and Takashi Matsushita, whom I called Mr. M. He was the father of one of my high school teammates and one of the first Japanese Americans—Nisei—to join the LAPD shortly after being in an internment camp during World War II. His son, George, was on the kickoff and receiving teams at Manual with me. George and I were close friends. His dad always treated me like family, and taught me, like he did George, the martial art of aikido; an extremely efficient defensive fighting technique that's used throughout Japan by their police. I had boxed at the Boys Club since I was nine years old, and being ambidextrous, I had power in both hands. At fourteen, when Mr. M started training me, a light turned on in my head. By fifteen, I was combining aikido with boxing. I called my style "boxido," and it was deadly. By eighteen, if I could get within three feet of a dude, it was lights-out. I always kept my shit close to the vest, and few knew of my fighting skills. But it was Mr. M's teachings of Bushido, the way of the warrior, that stuck with me. Bushido taught faith, indomitable spirit, and humility as ideals I strive to attain, and they've served me well.

It was Tyler who secured my orders to Naval District Washington after I rotated out of Japan and encouraged me to continue my education. By 1973, when I left the Navy, I had a civilian job at MIS. I was one of the first agents Tyler requested. When I think of all our history, I know this Goins thing has to be heavy for Tyler to ask me to wrap it up in this manner.

Denny and Rory come out of her office. Denny says, "Man, you think we got paperwork problems? You ought to see this woman's books!"

Rory fixes me another Jack, and as I light another Kool, she calls her shot. "Ricardo, you young but you not dumb. This GI is dead and quiet, so you let it lie. No Dick Tracy stuff."

"I dig you big, sis, but this shit is foul. If I was Goins, I wouldn't want to be swept under the rug. I'd want justice."

"Goins is with his God now. He don't want justice or anything else. Now let him rest in peace, Ricardo," Rory says sternly.

For the first time, I can see where Tyler is coming from. This investigation might turn up a boatload of BS, but it certainly won't help a dead man. And it might prolong his family's misery. Maybe he should rest in peace.

"Yeah, Rory, you got it right. I should let it go. There's always going to be more funky stuff around the corner in P.I. I just hate to leave a case half-done. Denny, I'll have my notes on your desk 0600 tomorrow, but I got a question for you."

"Shoot away."

"I ran into this dude named Franco at the embassy who reminded me of the description of that tech rep Zimmerman for some reason. Just a hunch: did you see a picture of this guy?"

"That's a 10-4, good buddy," Denny says.

"Well, what the hell did he look like?"

"Like a shithead college hippie—red Afro, big bushy beard, and John Lennon glasses. A regular Jerry Rubin, typical college pussy. Is that answer good enough?"

"Man, I had a theory going on, but that answer shot it all to hell. I guess this case is a dead end."

157

I finish my drink and head out to my barrio hooch to Nea. "Later on, y'all, take it light," I say as I leave.

"You, too, little brother," Rory says.

I get to our crib in about twenty minutes. Nea is in flip-flops and a bikini, ironing one of her trademark blue outfits while some her pancit canton noodle dish cooks on the stove.

"Ricky, I thought you butterfly on me with Manila girl. Glad you find your way home," Nea says in a mock-hurt voice.

"Hey, I ain't the only butterfly in this camp. Good for the goose, good for the gander," I laugh.

"Ricky, you just don't bring me any clap, and don't bring any little bitches to our hooch, and everything is okay. I've got to get to the club. Pancit is on the stove, you eat two balut because I horny, no shit." Nea chuckles.

Nea finishes ironing, gets dressed, kisses me ferociously, and hops in a Jeepney headed into Olongapo City. I grab a brew from the icebox and throw *Hank Mobley's Roll Call* on the system. This reminds me that my old buddy, Al Washington, an intel officer over at FICPAC, promised to put some of my Lee Morgan LPs on reel-to-reel tape. Papa Joe had a reel to reel, and that way he could play several sides without changing records whenever I had a Lee Morgan jones. I nod out, but as she warned me, Nea was hot as a firecracker and raring to go. Sparks were flying in the barrio that night.

The next morning, I woke up feeling like a million bucks. I quietly put some water on to boil to make my instant coffee, took a P.I. shower, got dressed, and had a morning smoke with my coffee. Nea was still in dreamland. I kissed her on the forehead and tiptoed out of the crib. I hopped a Jeepney to the back gate and made my way to HQ. I wanted to get my notes together for Denny. It was just after 0600 when I got to the shop, Denny was already there. He was at his desk going over his notes and the other intel we had gathered concerning Goins. I gave him my notes, got another cup of coffee, and sat down at my desk.

"Look, pard, this is the best thing, get this mess off the books. This wasn't no lynching, and Goins damn sure didn't shove that smack that far up his own ass, and this report is going to reflect that. Just a tragic death, a misadventure in P.I. Hopefully his family will get the survivor pay," Denny says.

"Yeah, man, but this case was starting to crack. I was getting a glimpse of a bigger picture—like a jigsaw puzzle, we're just missing a couple of key pieces," I reply.

"I hear you Ricky-san. But we can't solve every case. We just got to ruck up and fall in sometimes." When Denny said this, I knew that was the way it was.

By 0800 the shop was at full strength, and the skipper informed us of a huge typhoon—Olga—that had hit Guam and was making its way toward P.I. All ships, even the old sub, the USS Greyback, were being ordered out of Subic Bay. The base was battening down for the deluge. The naval base, air station, and its US citizens could withstand these storms. All their buildings were concrete block, the roads were well paved, and there were backup generators everywhere, but the town of Olongapo, the little country villages, and the big-city slums would be wiped out if a big storm hit. The half-assed switchback dirt roads would wash away, and many folks would die, mostly little kids and old people. It was during these disasters that I felt the US military provided its greatest service — that of humanitarian relief — supplying food, medicine, and rescue efforts, the Navy Seabees would assist in rebuilding roads and bridges. This was part of the price to pay for having a compliant tyrant like Marcos on your payroll. But the GI's that did the actual work of rebuilding knew in their hearts that they helped the needy in a time of great need. They put something back from where they usually only took. The storm was three to four days out, but I knew I had to give Nea a heads-up, so she could take care of her place in San Antonio. Tyler gave me the day off to get me out of the office and away from Denny. When I got back to the barrio, Nea was awake, drinking coffee and dragging on a Parliament, her favorite brand.

"Ricardo, why you home? Something the matter?"

I explain about the coming typhoon as I light up a Kool.

"You right, Ricky, I should go home. I'll get my girls, and we take Victory Liner back to Province. You come with us."

"No, doll, I got to stay put. I'll shack up on base. I'll batten our hooch down. You tell the neighbors about the storm."

I kept a couple watertight containers to

store some of our stuff, but the valuables like my stereo and Nea's sewing machine I would bring on base for safer storage. Nea told our landlords about the storm, and they spread the word through the Barrio. Nea and I agreed to meet at Papa Joe's that evening. She would leave for San Antonio the next day. I head back to base, this time to talk to KC at the photo lab. I remember the flicks of the pipe and pick them up. That, too, is a dead-end story. KC is back in the repair trailer working on a Leica M3 camera.

"Cap, what's going on? I thought you and Watash here was going to make a Manila run," he says.

"Oh, we gonna make that run bro, and Rolfie's Daktari Club is where we goin'. He's got some stone freaks up in that joint. But on the real side, I need you to do me a solid."

"Name it, Cap. It ain't nothing but a thing to do."

"I need to hold your ride for twenty-four or so. I got to get my loot from the Barrio back on base where it's nice and dry."

KC throws me the keys to his Land Rover and says, "Cap, you can store your gear here at the lab. I got a secure space behind this trailer."

"Thanks for the offer. But I'll stow my kit up at my quarters."

"Suit yourself, but my shit is totally watertight," KC says.

"Just like old Senior Chief's dome," I add.

"You got that right. Truck's out front. Don't fuck it up."

"Your ride is in good hands with Capone, dig?"

"Yeah, Daddy-O, I can dig it, but like I said—don't fuck up the truck."

I walked around the building to get the vehicle, an almost-new 1974 Land Rover that was the perfect ride for the fucked-up dirt roads of P.I.: four-wheel drive and built like a German tank. There was also a lot of room for gear. I figured two runs, max, and I'd have the hooch cleared out.

I drove off the base through the main gate, down Magsaysay, took a right on Rizal, and headed for the barrio. I managed to get all our gear, including the futon, into the Rover. Then, I opened the envelope from the photo lab. Along with the prints and negatives of the pipe, there was a color contact sheet of Goins' autopsy pictures. Right then and there, standing in the middle of my now-empty hooch, alone, I made up my mind that no MIS, Navy, US government, or even friends were going to stop me from getting to the bottom of Goins' murder. I decided I'm reopening this case on my own.

After getting our gear stowed on base, I drove out to the Green Dolphin to hook up with Nea. Papa Joe and Baby Sis were happy to see Nea and made her favorite concoction - a tequila sunrise made to her specs. Joe even laid off the hard bop and put on *Earth, Wind & Fire, Dionne Warwick,* and *George Benson*—sounds that Nea dug. We planned to stay on base this evening, then I'd take her and her home girls to the Victory Liner and send them off to San Antonio.

Papa Joe is sweet-talking my lady, trying to needle me. "Nea, you are a very maganda, young lady. Why do you put up with this scar-faced sand crab? Find yourself a nice CPO and move to California, sit home in AC, eat chocolates, and watch TV," Joe says.

"Papa, I been to USA already. They treat Filipina bad, and black worse. I'm staying right here in my homeland, and Ricky can stay with me. He's a good man, scar face and all," Nea says.

"Hear that you old goat, 'a good man.' Now quit your cock-blocking, and freshen us up for the road," I say.

Joe hooks us up as *Nancy Wilson* and *Cannonball Adderley* play low in the background. I realize how much Nea and Joe mean to me, and how comfortable I feel in their company. It's a feeling I've rarely had since 1957 when my mom passed away, and my own family basically dissolved.

We drove back on base and spent a quiet evening watching AFRTS[20] on my nineteen-inch Sony Trinitron. The next morning only Josie showed up, seems like Vilma was shacked up with a gunny sergeant on base. I dropped Nea and Josie at the Victory Liner and watched the kaleidoscope of humanity boarding the white buses with their red logos; well-dressed men and women, bar girls, babies, old-timers, peasants with chickens in bamboo cages—the whole nine yards. I watched as their bus pulled off, Nea and Josie waving and blowing me kisses.

---

[20] AFRTS – The American Forces Network

I drove by our hooch and put up heavy plywood over the doors and windows. After I'd battened down as well as I could, I drove back to the photo lab to return the Rover to KC

CHAPTER 12

It was a beautiful, cloudless, calm day when I woke up. The quiet before the storm. I went to the gym to pump some iron. I felt good and decided to take a run to cap off my workout. I had a five-mile course that included a long hill past the five-hundred-man marine camp down to Boton Wharf and back to my quarters. I was running, relaxed and loose, but at a six-minute mile clip. As I started to unwind, I felt good knowing that Nea would be with her people. Her blockhouse and generator could shelter quite a few folks. The road I ran cut right through the jungle. You could hear and see monkeys, all types of birds, and occasionally run across some monster snakes. AE1 Phil Goins was on my mind. It was weird that those flicks of Goins were included with the shots of that pipe. I guess Manny had that contact sheet and figured MIS might as well have it, too. I wondered if that jungle activity was somehow related to Goins' death, but I couldn't see any connection.

I was supposed to hook up with Al Washington later in the afternoon. At about 1700 hours, I headed to the married officers' quarters where Al and his family reside. It was near an eighteen-hole golf course that was very comfortable, like any middle-class suburb stateside. Al Washington was a sharp dude; he was a graduate of CCNY but was drafted all the same. He joined the Navy in 1959 and was a second-class PT working in CVIC when I met him on the Coral Sea in 1964, the only brother in that division, and one of the few in the Operations Department. We met during smokers in Yokosuka, we both made it to the 7th Fleet boxing semifinals. I lost on points to a marine from Okinawa, fighting as a light heavyweight. Al made it to the finals as a welterweight before he was defeated. We discovered that we both had some interest and skill in Japanese martial arts, he in karate-do and me with aikido. From that point on, we would often train and spar together. Al left the Coral Sea in early 1966 for OCS and became an intel officer.

Al's wife, Carol, had cooked up some Hoppin' John and collards to go with my favorite fried chicken livers. As Al and I begin to get down to the music, Carol calls in from the kitchen, "Ricky, I fixed you some up home Harlem soul food 'cause I know that rice-powered mama you're shacked up with can't burn like this.

You can't eat fish heads every day."

"Honey, one man's fish head is another man's caviar," Al says.

"Carol, I appreciate your efforts, and I'm gonna seriously grease to show my gratitude," I say.

"Well, go easy greasy, you got a long way to slide," Carol replies, adding, "Your little red schoolhouse is back stateside. Guess that's why you been scarce around here." Carol was referring to a middle-aged, brown-skinned, big-boned woman with red hair who happened to be a librarian named Doreen — my part-time lover.

"Now, Carol, you ain't telling me nothing, but she will return, and so will Ricky-san. There goes the neighborhood," I say. This gets a laugh from both Al and Carol.

Carol leaves to play Bid Whist at the rec center. The kids are out doing what teenagers do. It's just me and Al.

"Ricky, I see you got about eight LPs, probably forty to forty-five minutes of sound on each, depending on the quality you want. We can get four on a seven-inch reel at three and three-quarter speed that should be plenty of quality for Papa Joe's system," Al says.

"Hey, man, you the recording engineer—I'm just the DJ," I say.

"Okay, DJ, pick 'em. Let's have your top four."

I picked out *Sidewinder*, *Cornbread*, *The Gigolo*, and a Japanese pressing of a live concert at the Lighthouse in LA called *Speedball*. Al fixed me a Jack and got a Budweiser for himself. Al was a light drinker, never hard liquor, but I knew he would tip a couple of brews with me. The recording started, and we talked of our days on the Coral Sea, families, and plans. I told him some of the facts of the Goins case and my recruitment by the State Department boys, and about the Frogs.

"Ricky, let me school you on some things: the military, the agencies, the State Department, the Peace Corps, mercs like the Frogs—they're all tools to extend US economic interests worldwide. Our employer is the US Military-Industrial Complex."

"Okay, Al. So, what you saying?"

"Ricky, what I'm saying is that it's the system we're part of. At the low end is the grunt in the boonies with a M16. At the high end are the big-time bankers, industrialists, and diplomats. Outside of that, there's the commies, the third world, and the poor worldwide—from our city ghettos to the shit-pile hovels around here. These cats that have been rapping to you are the point men of the US power structure." *Lee* was wailing at a low volume in the background as Al continued, "After Nam fell, the Soviets filled the void we left, getting a ready-made warm-water port. The red Chinese grabbed up the golden triangle, and the US is out in the cold. My feeling is the US is going to play China against the Soviets, with China and the US as partners. That's called realpolitik."

"Man, that's some heavy shit, but I've done enough cowboy stuff for a lifetime or two. And us and the Chi Com—I can't see it," I say.

"The world is fluid, Ricky. Thirty-five years ago, Japan and Germany were our deadly enemies. Today, they are our biggest trading partners. In another thirty-five years, who knows what will go down with China. As the saying goes, 'The enemy of your enemy is your friend.'"

I finished my Jack, and Al puts the last LP on his Denon turntable, carefully removing the dustcover from the album and then laying stylus to vinyl.

"Ricky, pour yourself another hit. I just keep that Tennessee oil for my old friends like you. Grab me a Bud and let me pontificate to you some more."

"Rap on, Professor, but I don't want to stifle your family scene."

"Not a problem, Ricky, Carol's got her Bid Whist club, and Saturday night is the only night I give the kids liberty. We got till 2400."

We drink and shoot the bull as *Speedball* plays through. I hand Al the other albums, *Search for the New Land*, *Leeway*, *Candy*, and *Night of the Cookers*—an all-out blowing session with *Lee* and *Freddie Hubbard* live in NYC. Al was as meticulous in his recording methods as with everything else he did: his job, family, and appearance. AL was always AJ squared-away. He was about five foot seven, with a wiry frame, dark skin, graying short hair, and a trim goatee. Many people resented Al because of his clean-cut and mild manner, but all respected him, including the mostly white officers and men he worked with. He was above reproach. As we settled into round two of the recording session, Al lays some more of his worldview on me.

"Thing is, Ricky, our enemies today could well be our allies tomorrow. All this Cold War okeydokey is really about which economic system will call the shots: our supposed democracy, or the Soviets' so-called communism."

"Yeah, Al, but why does it have to get down to blowing folks away halfway across the globe?"

"Hearts and minds, baby. We got to show that we can go toe-to-toe with those commies. So, the developing world will dance to our tune. In the end, capitalism will win. No developed countries ever bought in to that commie jive, just poor peasant farmers in Nam, China, Cuba, and Russia. But let them get industrialized and they'll want two cars and color TV's, just like in the US. Communism goes against the basic human instinct of greed. In thirty or forty years, the US government is betting everyone will be buying American goods and services worldwide. That's why cats are getting shot up, bro."

"So, it's like my boy Romeo says, 'Money talks and bullshit walks.'"

"Yeah, Ricky, always been so, from the rice paddy to the White House. Them that gots the gold, rule."

"So, why you runnin' this shit down on me, Al?"

"Because, my man, I see you questioning your job and what you're doing, and I'm telling you the system's too big to beat. Just do what you can for you and yours, and try to pull another brother up, but pick your battles well, and know the cards are stacked against you."

We settle into the last album, *Leeway*, and I'm into my fourth tumbler of Jack on ice. Al's sipping a soda pop now. It seems as if Al just looked through me and saw my dilemma with this Goins case and in his own intellectual way was saying what everyone else had already said - let Goins rest in peace and move on to the next case.

Shortly after midnight, Carol and the kids got back home. I said good-bye, and Al gave me and my music a ride to my quarters in his spotless Toyota Corona.

CHAPTER 13

The storm hit hard that Sunday afternoon. It rained nonstop buckets of water for three days. Small villages and dirt roads were washed away, and many people died as a result of Typhoon Olga. On the American military bases, the sturdy concrete buildings and ample electric power allowed the US forces to remain largely intact. By Thursday, the ships started to return to Subic Bay, and rebuilding and aid efforts were in full swing. As for Denny B and myself, we got some time off to square away our personal shit.

"Ricky, that was a downright deluge we just survived. I got Rory on base with me, and Peanuts, but she's anxious as a one- eyed cat at a fish market, worrying 'bout her joint," Denny says.

"Hey, man, the woman's club is her castle. Nea went back to San Antonio to be with her folks. I've got to check on her club myself."

"How you figure your hooch held up?"

"Well, we only got three rooms, and we're uphill on a concrete slab. I got plywood over the doors and windows, and all the good stuff is at the base. I guess we're cool, I'll know for sure pretty soon."

"Well, shipmate, you need a lift to your place?" Denny asks.

"No, D.B., I'm gonna walk the main drag and survey the damage, then check on Nea's Club."

"Suit yourself. I'll ride you out to Gordon Street."

"You got it, man."

Denny and I got into his Ford pickup and headed out of the gate. Denny had some knee-high rubber boots on. I had a pair of old waders on, and it was a good thing. As we exited the base, the first block of Magsaysay, which was below street level, was wiped out by standing water. All the little beer gardens destroyed. I hopped out at Gordon Street, which, along with the rest of the main drag, were just muddy trenches.

Just as before Olga hit, today was a perfectly clear, blue-sky sunny day. Folks were busy cleaning up. Most of the big clubs on the main drag were on the second levels and sustained minimal damage. But the smaller bars, tailor shops, cobblers, and the like were on ground level, and some were hard hit. Nea's club was on the ground level, and when I got to her joint,

Club Misty Blue, I was expecting the worst. But after opening the padlocked door, I found the joint not too much the worse for wear. There were a couple inches of water on the deck, and the pleather-covered bar had some water damage, but Nea and her crew had stashed almost everything else in a small second-floor storage room.

I got started with a squeegee and swab, and after a couple of hours had the place dry and, with the help of some pine oil, smelling fresh. I spotted Jackson and had him bring me a couple cold San Miguels. I sat in the open doorway of the Misty Blue, letting it air out. After my lunch break, I brought the chairs and tables down and got the club squared away. I left the booze locked up in a footlocker and stacked the two cases of warm San Miguels behind the bar. Hopefully the electricity would be restored soon, and Olongapo City would be back in business. I re-padlocked the door and left the little club thinking how happy Nea would be with my handiwork. I walked down the main drag until I got to Papa Joe's, where I heard *Louis Armstrong's "West End Blues"* blasting out the Dolphin's windows and down the street.

"What you know, Pops?" I holler.

"Juney! It's good to get a sniff of you, boy. How's that fine lady of yours?"

"She went home to San Antonio, they didn't get hit as hard as we did. She got word back to the shop that she's okay and will be back here as soon as the roads are drivable."

"You hear I got *Louis* playing. This big wind that just blew through here reminds me of a Crescent City blow, and I'm playing pops in its wake."

"I guess that's why *Louie* could blow so hard. God put that big wind in his lungs."

"You got that right, son. Hey, pour yourself a hook. I appreciate you looking in, but me and mines are cool, high and dry with electricity."

I pour a couple of fingers of Jack and light up a Kool. Joe and I play some dominoes in almost total silence. In the background, Armstrong is playing with his hot seven, but at a much lower volume. Papa Joe and I didn't have to say a word. We knew we were there for each other, rain or shine.

After leaving Papa Joe's, I made my way down

Rizal and caught one of the few Jeepneys that were out and about and made my way back to our crib. I passed Smitty's place and saw him and a now–visibly pregnant Celi, hanging stuff out to dry. I hollered and waved, and they waved back with big smiles. When I reached our place and opened the padlocked door, I found not a bit of damage. Just lucky, I guess.

Within a week or so, the base and Olongapo City were back to situation normal: work hard, play harder. This was the Summer doldrums for the Subic area. There was no carrier group scheduled in for a couple of months. The Connie was due back before returning to its home port of North Island, and the Ranger wasn't due in until late December. Some smaller CG's[21] and destroyers were in and out, and the old sub Greyback and the USS Jason were tied up at Boton Wharf, along with several thousand sailors and marines lucky enough to be stationed in P.I.

It was during these slow times that Subic Bay and Olongapo City resembled an army post or air-force base with the same GIs working on base and partying in town, day after day. Many of these stationditos had steady girlfriends,

---

[21] CG's – Cruisers

clubs they frequented, and cribs in PO Town; they were regular working stiffs. Many of the working girls would return to their home provinces during these slow times. Once the big-carrier task force returned, Olongapo would gear up for the quick cash that the fleet sailors brought with them. This was quite a ratcheting down from the ten previous years during Vietnam when ships were in and out of Subic Bay on a hot-and-heavy basis. Olongapo was adapting to the peacetime Navy.

Nea came back after I had field-dayed the club and hooch. I took a couple of days off to help her get everything back together. It was the first Monday in June when I reported into work and found the going very mundane.

"Morning, morning, young Ricardo. And how are you this fine Navy day?" Denny says as I walk into HQ.

"Denny, I'm as happy as a pimp with a bag full of pussy," I reply.

"Well, son, that means Miss Nea must have put the hammer down on your young ass last night."

"You got that right. I think my nose is getting open just thinking about it."

"Well, pard, us old folks can rock and roll, too. Rory laid it on me heavy. I wonder if those birds are in cahoots—you know, fuck us till our minds get stuck in neutral, then spend our paychecks at the BX."

"You know, D.B., Nea did mention coming on base today."

Tyler called muster[22] and went over the status of pending cases, which for us in the criminal division was minimal, just some teenage vandalism and the usual petty crime. The Goins case wasn't mentioned. Yesterday's news swept under the rug.

"Gents, it's slow right now, and the next big carrier group doesn't arrive for a while, but this is still P.I., and there's always something simmering, about to boil over. Right now, catch up on your reports, maybe check in on your families. To that end, we're going port and starboard until further notice."

A loud cheer goes up.

"Now you're talking, Skip!" Greevy, a middle-aged white agent from Boston says.

"Okay, Greevy, you, Denny, Ricky, and Octavio

---

[22] Muster – A formal gathering of troops

are starboard; White, Collins, Wilson, and Taylor are port. All right you - ports, shove off. Rick, let me have a word in my office," Tyler says.

I follow him into his office. "Shut the door, Rick. Take a seat. Look, I know this Goins case has become a crusade for you, but we were ordered from way up to close it out. The man was dead, and the top brass wanted him put to bed."

"I hear you, Skip, but I thought there's a lot more to this case than meets the eye. Morris at the embassy told me I could have some more time to snoop it through and see where it led."

"Well, Rick, it led to Denny's report, and that's what we passed up the chain. I've known you for years, and you've always known when to throw down your cards and move on. Now is one of those times."

"Hey, Skip, I've already blown that pop stand."

"Good, Rick, 'cause you know some shit's always about to hit the fan here in Subic, and I need you on your A game."

"You know it's 100 percent with me, Skip."

"Okay, Rick, get your paperwork squared away, and any qualifications you need to bring up to date. Also, Rick, I want you to look into that master's program at the University of Maryland extension; a little challenge might get your head right."

As I left Tyler's office, I knew my head wouldn't be right until I closed out this Goins thing, but I would put it on the back burner for now. And just as Tyler had predicted, it wasn't long before some new shit royally hit the fan.

CHAPTER 14

The Commander has been meeting with the twelve-year-old hooker for a couple of months. He's broken down the girl's defenses with liquor and gifts and has explored every inch of her body with his hands and mouth. He had her lick his feet as he masturbated, but he had not had actual intercourse with her yet. But today along with his vodka "Kool-Aid" and a beautiful white dress, he bought some KY jelly to facilitate his intentions.

After walking several blocks on Gordon Street, he walks into a dilapidated three-story apartment building, goes upstairs to room 211, turns the doorknob, and enters a small room. It's filled with dolls and toys. On the double bed in a pink pinafore with white socks and patent-leather shoes is the young girl, with her angelic face and vacant, dead eyes.

"Hello, little princess, look what Papa's brought you today."

"Salamat Po[23]," the girl replies in a flat monotone voice.

"Come over here to Papa. Let's have a Kool-Aid and admire your new dress." The Commander

---

[23] Salamat Po – Thank you sir

lays the white dress at the foot of the bed. He removes his ball cap and aviator glasses as he pours the girl some of his "joy juice." Within a few minutes, he has removed her pinafore and underwear, but left her shoes and socks on. He is hungrily licking her small, thin body. She is completely nonresponsive: she has a glazed zombie-like expression on her face and is totally silent. He plies her with another cup of his Kool-Aid and proceeds to apply the KY jelly to her private parts. As he attempts to initiate intercourse, the girl lets out a loud scream. This infuriates the Commander, who pins her down on the bed and mounts her slender, small body. Her screams become desperate and chilling, he covers her mouth and nose with a large hand. As he enters her, she struggles and tries to bite him. He slaps her hard on the side of the head, her body then convulses spasmodically and becomes still. He withdraws from the girl and watches her eyes roll back into her head as blood hemorrhages from her sex organs. The bed is soon soaked in bright red blood. The Commander cannot revive her. In a cool, calm manner, he dresses and squares himself away, picks up both dresses and underwear, puts them back into the bag, along with his container of Kool-Aid, puts his Ray-Bans on, and slinks out of room 211 while she bleeds to death.

Unbeknownst to the Commander, the girl's screaming had roused Mumbles, the old hooker from VP Alley who lives in the building. In half a stupor, she looks out her door just in time to see the Commander fleeing the scene, putting his cap on. Mumbles walks to room 211 and opens the door. The sight that greets her sends her into a fit of hysterical screaming.

"What the fuck kind of shit is this, D.B.?" I ask upon walking into room 211, where Tyler and Denny are standing in the midst of dolls, toys, and a dead girl on a blood-soaked bed, naked except for white bobby sox and black patent-leather shoes. Her beautiful face looks almost peaceful, except for her eyes, which are rolled back into her skull.

"Pard, I don't know what the hell this is, but it don't take a lot of imagination to speculate. That old rummy down the hall claims to have seen a GI—tall, bald officer, no less—leave the room," Denny says.

"Now, how the fuck would that old boozehound know who the perp was?" I ask.

"Rick, Mumbles has been in Olongapo since

Moby Dick was a minnow. Drunk or not, she's seen damned near every swinging dick that's walked these streets for thirty years or more, and she's raising hell about this perverted shit being committed by an American officer. Ernie and the PC are here, also, but the locals are getting fired up. We need to contain this ASAP," Tyler says.

Tyler was right. A group of Filipinos had responded to Mumbles' screams and saw what I had just seen in room 211, and they were incensed to the point of riot. PC, shore patrol, and MIS were all on the scene trying to keep this powder keg from blowing, while gathering evidence at the same time.

Smitty was the duty photog, and he looks over at me and says, "Rick, I hope I never see anything like this again."

"Yeah, me, too, Smitty." I think back to the kids that I had seen killed by bombs or napalm in Nam. Blown to bits and burnt up, but this was a different bag. Bombs are indiscriminate; they destroy all in their path: people, animals, plants, even their own soldiers. This here was outright murder by perversion. Ernie's PC boys were managing to contain the angry mob to the point of something close to order.

Tyler spoke to Octavio, Denny, Greevy, and me, who had caught duty that day.

"Gents, we're out here at this death scene, that was witnessed by nobody, because that old sea hag over there is insisting that an American officer left the scene. Her description is sketchy at best: tall, white, bald, slim, maybe forty or so, wearing aviator glasses. Hell, there could be a couple hundred guys fill that bill. But she's got the PC, and now Mayor Horton on the warpath. They contacted the Provost Marshal, and now we're here to investigate. We can't assume anything. Let's try to get as much intel as we can now, before the scene becomes too degraded."

"Well, Skip, we know we got a dead little girl here, and she damned sure don't look like she was working for herself. So, there's a Mamasan or Papasan involved with this shit, too. A lot of shitheads could get caught in this dragnet," Denny says.

"That's true enough, D.B., but let's approach it like this: We police our side of the street and let the PC keep Olongapo's citizens in check," Tyler says.

"So, what is it, Skip?" I ask.

"Rick, you and me will give the crime scene a closer look before the morgue boys disturb anything. Keep that photog here so he can shoot flicks to our specs. Denny, you run Gordon Street, sniff around and see who might be running a kiddie show around here. Octavio, you and Greevy check Mumbles out when you can get her alone. We need a good, clean translation of all that she thinks she saw and heard. This could run late, but I want everyone at muster tomorrow for a debrief."

We all acknowledge our orders and go about carrying them out. Tyler and I are going over room 211. He remarks, "damn sure looks like a GI was involved. These baby dolls and dresses look to be straight out of the BX. Photog—get some snaps of all these toys and clothes and try to get some pictures before the forensic guys close the girl's eyes."

"Aye, aye, Mr. Tyler," Smitty replies.

We find the paper cup with the vodka Kool-Aid in it. Maybe we could lift a print from the cup. We put the liquid in a small container and bag the cup. Tyler, Smitty, and I are all wearing cotton gloves. Except for the mess on the bed, the room is very clean. This sicko had a cool head. But he may have made a mistake in his getaway. Under the bed I find a receipt from the BX in Cubi Point for forty-two US dollars.

"Hey, Skip, I think this clown might have tripped up," I say.

We gathered what evidence we could from the room, and Smitty shot at least three rolls of 35 mm film on his Nikon camera. The receipt was the only solid lead we'd been able to take away from the scene.

I got home to the barrio well past curfew, completely exhausted and mentally drained. The sight of that young girl who died so violently had me shook up. I poured myself a couple of fingers of Makers and fired up a Kool, as I sat in almost total darkness I thought, that little girl was the same age as my baby sisters. This is the down side of police work; what you all too often see is the slimy side of life.

Nea came out of the bedroom and looked at me sitting in the darkness and asked, "What's the matter, Rick? You look like you saw a ghost."

"Worse, honey, I saw what the devil creates."

I told Nea about the crime scene. She came and put her arms around my shoulders and gently kissed my scarred cheek. She put me to bed like I was eight years old, holding me tight until

I nodded off. The next morning, in addition to the loud-ass roosters crowing, I was awakened by the smell of bacon frying and coffee percolating. Hearing that bacon crackle made me think of my mom's Sunday breakfasts all those years ago. Watching Nea burn at the stove made me wonder if her circumstances had been different, would she have been a nurse or a teacher. I also wondered what that dead girl could have been had adults not valued her life so cheaply.

"Ricky, you were tossing and turning all night, but you still stay sound asleep. I couldn't get any sleep, so I decided to make you a good breakfast. Then we talk."

"Talk about what, doll?"

After she fixes my plate, Nea sits down with a cup of coffee and lights a Parliament and starts telling me her story.

"Ricky, I go to work for Mamasan at twelve years old in Angeles City. I clean up for hostess, do laundry, clean out rooms, and watch GIs give girls money, VD, and sometimes beatings. When I'm fifteen, my body full grown, GI like me, and I like money and GIs, especially soul brothers, so I become hostess. But Ricky, I'm lucky girl. Many other young girls and boys—seven, eight years old—have no family and become sex slave. Young children bring the most money for Mamasan."

"Nea, you never told me this stuff. What's up?"

"Ricky, you never asked. It's like your scar."

"Right on honey, some shit is need-to-know I guess."

"Ricky, what you need to know is no one turned me out. I make my own mind up, but these little kids have no choice or chance. For most GI, P.I. is fun with grown women, but for a few it's a sickness with kids and big money."

"You know, Nea, I knew this shit went on, but like everyone else, I looked the other way. But that dead girl in those little shoes with those dolls has got me all fucked-up. I want to find the piece of shit that did this and break every bone in his body before he gets hanged."

"Ricky, you find him and let others judge him. But what happened last night happens every day around the world. Maybe all kids don't die, but they are already dead inside. Here in P.I., any Yankee round-eye can buy a kid. Like Romeo says, 'Money talks.'"

Nea and I eat our breakfast. I wash up and

192

dress for work. Nea crawls back in the rack for some shut-eye without me to flip and flop and keep her awake.

I arrive at HQ and at 0800 on the dot, Tyler calls muster to go over the events of the previous night for the port-section boys who were off duty. Then calls for a debrief.

"All right, gents, let's see where we stand. Octavio, what did you and Greevy find out from Ichiban boozehound?"

Octavio responds in his clipped but careful English, "Well, Mr. Tyler, Mumbles was half-stewed as always, but she says that this tall, white GI has been visiting this girl in room 211 for six to eight weeks. Seems like the pattern is fairly consistent. The girl arrives, and about a half hour later, GI Joe shows up."

Greevy picks up the story, "The old twist kept mentioning Ten High. We thought she meant bourbon, but she meant a little hole in the wall over by the east end. I checked it out, while Octavio continued to grill Mumbles. Nothing but a dive, a couple old salts and some vintage 1955 hookers. The Mamasan's name was Conception Ramos, heavyset broad about thirty-five to forty. When I asked about real young hookers, she looked at me and played dumb."

"Okay, Denny, what do you know?" Tyler asks.

"Skip, it seems like that Ten High, along with Mariposa Club, are known for real young girls. Now, this Mariposa is right on Gordon Street, so I went by for a sniff. The youngest broad I saw was about seventeen, and there was a dozen or so others in that age range, along with a group of E5 and below hippie-dippy hair-parted-in-the-middle squids. Thing is, my old lady mentioned the name Conception as a kiddie pimp."

"All right, this Ten High and Miss Ramos need to be pressed. Let's at least ID the girl before we turn this one over," Tyler says.

Tyler tells the men about the receipt I found, then gives us our new marching orders. "Needless to say Gents, this case has the potential to be a real powder keg. We saw that little girl, and if Mumbles is right and a naval officer is the perp, then that's one more reason for the anti-US Filipinos to demand our departure."

"Yeah, Skip, but Mumbles is crazy as a shithouse rat. Why are we giving her any credence at all?" Denny asks.

"'Cause that crazy rat's trap has been flapping, and now we're all involved. So, here's where we're at today, Denny, you check out the Ten High. Octavio, you and Greevy run Mumbles' down. Ricky, you head up to Cubi and track that receipt. Port Section, you hold down the fort. Okay, gents, carry on," Tyler finishes up and returns to his office.

White, Collins, Taylor and Wilson, the port section, are shaking their heads and commenting on the case.

"If I catch that sumbitch, I'll nail his nuts to a stump and watch him bleed out," Collins, a white agent in his mid-thirties, remarks.

"Roger that, Collins. That slime needs some stretching," Mark Wilson, a young black agent, says.

"Quell that BS, fellas. Let's just ID the vic and perp first before we convene a kangaroo court," Denny says.

CHAPTER 15

The exchange at Cubi Point opened at 1000. I arrived there at around 1030. I found the manager, a guy named Jimmy Delgado, a big Italian guy with an outgoing personality and a heavy scent of Old Spice. After I showed Delgado my badge, I showed him a photo of the receipt we'd found. Delgado studied it and said it was from register five, and the cashier's name was Liz Vega. He had no idea what the forty-two dollars had purchased.

"Liz is working today. Maybe she can give you more info."

"Okay, Mr. Delgado, let's talk to Miss Vega," I say.

We walked from Mr. Delgado's office through the Sansui and Kenwood stereo systems, Sony color TVs, Johnston & Murphy and Bally shoes, Omega and Rolex watches—all top-shelf stuff that even an enlisted man could afford. The exchange was a class A testament to the Yankee consumer. Everything in this world and then some at cut-rate prices. A sailor could do a lot worse than be stationed in the P.I. in 1976, where everything from a Rolex watch to a piece of tail was for sale at discount. This included young children, just another commodity for the rich Yankees.

When we got to Liz at register five, Delgado told her who I was and what I was after. I hadn't told Delgado any details of the investigation, just that this receipt was part of it. Liz Vega was around fifty, with a round, plump face and a nice smile. After looking at the photocopy, she acknowledged that it was indeed from her register.

"This receipt is three weeks old, but I think I remember this item. It was a fancy dress for a little girl. I remember, because I thought it would look nice on my granddaughter."

"Do you remember who bought the dress, Miss Vega?"

"Oh, yes, Filipina woman, maybe thirty or so."

"Do you know her? What did she look like?"

"I had never seen her before. Maybe five foot three, short hair, nice clothes, dependent ID."

"You should be a cop; you've got a hell of a memory. Can you remember a name?"

"Sorry, I'm drawing a blank there."

"Thank you for your time. If anything else comes to mind please contact me," I say, handing her one of my cards.

I thank Delgado and head to the CPO club for lunch. As I walked to the Top of the Mark, I had a feeling that my end of this case was a dead end, the only light being that the receipt was for a dress for a young girl. Maybe the Filipina who bought it was married to this sicko that Mumbles saw.

As I mull this intel around, I order a burger and brew from Benny, the CPO club bartender. There's a lot of laughter and jonesing going on at the table in the rear of the club. Two older black CPOs and a white dude of about the same age are playing cards and sipping mixed drinks.

"Mac, you one lucky so-and-so. Where did your red ass learn to play cards?" Master Chief JC Lanier asks.

"JC, I'm from Gary, Indiana, and I been playing tonk since I was a teenager working in the mills," Mac says.

"That's what it is, Mac; you been around us colored folk so long you even play cards like us," JC says. All these men are laughing now.

I call Benny over and ask him who the white dude is. Benny informs me he's a tech rep name of Jack McMillan. No, shit, I think to myself. One door closes and another opens.

"Hey, Benny, send those fellas another round," I say.

"Okay, Ricky. That's three seven-and-seven on your tab," Benny replies.

A waitress brings the drinks to the card players and points back toward me. The trio tips their glasses to me, I raise my brew in return, and say, "Hey, Mac, we got a mutual friend—Mike Zimmerman. Can I have a word?"

"Yeah, okay. Let me finish these birds off, and I'll give you a minute."

The men resume their card game and drinks. At about 1300, the two CPOs leave smiling and slapping Mac on the back.

Lanier says, "Mac, don't do nothing I wouldn't do. But if you do, name it after me, you hear."

"JC, you can put book on that," Mac says as he walks over to my barstool. "You want to talk about that prime sumbitch Zimmerman, huh?"

"Mac, I'm Ricardo Baptiste with the MIS Subic. I contacted you earlier this year about Phil Goins death."

"Okay, but I gave you guys a written statement.

Hell, I was back in CONUS when that went down, and I need to ID you before I do any singing."

I show my ID and badge. He jots down my name and number—typical detail-oriented twidget.

"What can you tell me about Goins and Zimmerman?"

"Like I said in my statement, Goins was a sharp AE1 - black kid at that. We were training these VRC 45 boys on the prowler. Goins took to hanging out with Zimmerman and these two big, tall hookers. Zimmerman had some rooms over at the Royal. I just figured they were into some kinky shit, but I can't guess why a kid like that would turn up dead in P.I."

"What about Zimmerman? What did he look like? What was his background? Had you two worked together previously?"

"He was a little shorter than you, maybe five nine or ten, curly reddish hair, bushy beard, John Lennon glasses—typical East Coast shit-for-brains college boy. I figured him to be a bean counter from Long Island because he didn't know squat about aircraft. But that hippie knew how to party."

"You all finished training before Thanksgiving?"

"Well, I left on December 2, Zimmerman split around Thanksgiving. But Goins caught yellow fever and took his leave in P.I. with one of those big broads. Damn, man, he had a wife and kids. And look where that oriental gash got him—pushing daisies."

"You're sure Zimmerman was some kind of accountant?"

"They said he was a technical manager, but the only thing technical about that bird was his daddy was technically rich, probably played golf with the CEO."

"You said he was a prime SOB. Why's that?"

"Well, he was an arrogant prick, and 'prime' was his favorite adjective: prime cars, prime pussy, prime pot. That's another thing—both Zimmerman and Goins were potheads. I can't truck that wacky tobaccy."

"Mac, thanks a lot. Can I contact you if something else turns up?"

"It's your dime, pal." We exchange business cards, and Mac splits. I order another brew.

On Gordon Street at Club Nuevo, Denny has a

C&C in front of him. Rory had done his legwork on the Ten High Club. Through her many contacts she got the straight skinny on Conception Ramos. The Ten High Club was a front for a thriving kiddie-sex business. Young boys and girls could be rented, but only for top dollar, one to two hundred US, depending on the time involved and the age of the child. According to Rory, Ramos had a barracks of ten to twenty kids out in Subic City that could be dispatched to service her clientele. The kids were all between eight and twelve years old.

"Now, baby, you're telling me this scumbag Mamasan has a house full of baby hookers out in Subic City," Denny says.

"That's right, honey, everyone knows about her business. But she is never with the kids. They're transported to the hookup spots."

"So, where is this piece-of-shit excuse for a woman at now? I'm going to bust her and her joint down most ricky ticky."

"Not so fast, hopalong. Miss Ramos took a powder. Vamoosed. And the Ten High is just another club. No kids inside."

"Well, baby, I'll tell you what. We're headed out to Subic City and find that kiddie bunkhouse,"

Denny says.

Meanwhile, Octavio and Greevy found Mumbles' at VP Alley drinking Johnny Walker and wearing a new Seiko watch. When Octavio begins questioning her, she looks at him as if the events of the last twenty-four hours were part of a Grimm Brothers' fairy tale.

"I no see nothing, no dead girl, no GI. You full of shit. You work for GI. You no real Filipino, you *baklat*!" Mumbles hisses at Octavio, who can tell by the way she's knocking back the Johnny Walker that he'll get nothing more out of her this day.

Octavio and Greevy look up two more of the flophouse bystanders and get the same reaction. No one knows a damned thing. Both men smell a cover-up.

Denny and Rory take Denny's F100 out to Subic City, a little town right out of a spaghetti western, with clubs named; The Good, The Bad, and The Ugly, My Other Place, and Stumpy and Gimpy's, lining a half-assed main drag. There are plenty of girls running around in cutoffs and wearing flip-flops on their wide peasant feet. Most of these women had ass for sale or rent. Rory and Denny are walking around like tourists, Rory in a sundress striking poses, Denny snapping pictures.

After a few San Miguels in a couple of the clubs, Rory gets a bead on Conception Ramos's dormitory. Denny and Rory walk up a dirt road about a quarter mile off the main street and come upon a one-story building that looks as if it could have been a horse stable at one time. There was a small concrete courtyard with about five or six ten- to twelve-year-old kids kicking a well-worn soccer ball around. Denny pretends to shoot pictures of Rory, meanwhile he's actually shooting the hovel and the kids. All of a sudden, a toothless old crone walks out of the building and runs the kids back inside. She screams at Denny,

"Yo! Ziggy na, I call P.C.! These my grandkids."

"No pictures?" Denny asks

"You go to hell, GI, and take your whore with you."

Having gotten the pictures, Denny and Rory have a beer at The Good, The Bad, and The Ugly before returning to Olongapo.

At quarters the next day, the photos of room 211 and the dead girl bled out on that funky mattress had everyone uptight again. After

Octavio, Denny, and I debriefed Tyler and the port section, he laid it on us. The case was disintegrating before our eyes.

"This case is over for MIS. Turn your notes over to me, and I'll put a report together. But the status is this: we got a dead girl of an unknown age in Olongapo City, P.I. Mumbles and others who saw the room got a case of the 'can't remember shit,' and Mamasan skipped town. As far as the US military is concerned, this is a Filipino problem. We're off the case, gents."

There was much grumbling and god damning among the men, and Denny spoke up, saying, "Tyler, we all saw that little girl bled out like a stuck pig. She didn't do that to herself. Mumbles' was telling the truth before someone bought her off, and I'll give you ten to one that this perp was some scumbag GI. Me and my lady friend saw a little kiddie farm out in Subic City, I took a few flicks. What the hell are we doing here?"

"Denny, you and Ricky been sounding like the bleeding-hearts club band lately. We're the Military Investigative Service, and our military boss, Vice Admiral Killian, says shut this one down. The PC got it from here on out, and that's the name of that tune.

"Denny, I'll give you ten to one that your kiddie farm is as empty as Bozo the Clown's head right about now," Tyler says grimly.

"All of this non-investigating we're doing here is starting to stink. We gonna sweep everything under the rug this year? First Goins, now this little girl. What's up, Skip?" I ask. At that, the tone of Tyler's voice becomes frosty.

"Look, gents, I don't like this call any more than you do. That kid looked like my girls did at that age. But we got our marching orders, and it is what it is."

"Okay, Tyler, so where do we stand now?" Greevy asks.

"Glad you asked, Greevy. We got a couple cases ongoing involving the package store that port section is handling, and the Connie and her battle group will be returning to Subic in about three weeks. So, we'll come off port and starboard when the Connie arrives."

"Okay, y'all can shove off. Octavio and Greevy, you got a report to put together. You two bleeding hearts - let me get your notes."

Denny and I walk to our desks in silence, get our notes together, and give them to Tyler. For the rest of the morning, I take my coffee like Denny, with a shot of C.C in it. We were both pissed at what had just transpired. At noon Denny looked in Tyler's office and asked if he and I could knock off early as there was nothing happening, and we were all caught up on our paperwork.

"Okay, Denny, you two go ahead and hit the beach. And next time I see you gents, let's try to have a better attitude," Tyler says.

"Right, Skip, we're already working on that attitude adjustment," Denny says as he leaves Tyler's office.

"Come on, pard, Skip says for us malcontents to hit the beach," Denny says to me.

We walk to Denny's pickup and head to the main gate.

"Hey, D.B., drop me by Papa Joe's. I need to mellow out and think some shit through. Man, you was starting to sound like me at quarters today."

"Yeah, even an old shit-kicker like me can smell the BS sometimes. But we just got to press on, pard."

"Right on, D.B. Be proud, be professional, and press on, that's the Navy way, baby."

Denny drops me at the Green Dolphin. I walk upstairs into the cool, clean sanctuary of jazz in Olongapo. Papa Joe, being a retired marine, could buy much Yankee-made gear for his joint; air conditioners, refrigerators, and even a backup generator—stuff that only the real big Olongapo clubs like Foxy's or the High Plains had. But no club had the bottled distilled water that Papa Joe used for his ice cubes, which is why Joe's drinks were the best in P.I., bar none.

"Juney, where you been at, boy? I caught *Miss Dionne Warwick* in Manila awhile back, man. That hammer is long, tall, fine, and sings like a nightingale," Joe says upon seeing me.

There are three or four regulars in the club, along with Lettie, Baby Sis, a couple of bar girls, and Starchild. They're all laughing at stuff in a comic book. *Wes Montgomery* is on the system, and I'm getting mellow already. Joe pours me a stout hook of Jack over ice and says, "Hey, son, I know about that little girl. Ernie ran that game down to me. You dig, son? Some games are too big to be messed with."

"Pops, what the hell you talking about? I didn't say a damned thing about no girl or game."

"Juney, I know what's rattling around in your head. You think you can make shit right, give that dead girl some justice, make the world better. But dig, son, she was part of a world that puts a price on everything, and unless you're on top, you will get fucked over one way or another. You dig?"

"Yeah, I hear you, Pops, but that don't make that shit right. Sometimes I just want to say fuck all this BS and live in the desert by my damn self."

"Hey, son, I got out of the rat race. I live here. Don't mess with nobody, take care of me and mines, and spread the gospel of Jazz, but I can't get away from the world and the foul shit in it. Everything is everything. We just got to deal with it, take life on life's terms, and keep the faith. Juney, you listen to your inner voice, and the Creator will tell you how to live."

"Pops, you going spiritual on me now?"

"Son, that's what life is about, finding your place in the world and being a part of life. My concept of life changed in 1950 when I was thirty-five years old. I was in Korea up above the 47th parallel, and we were getting tore up by the Chinese and North Korean regulars.

Back at that time I had the kill mentality, I had got used to killing. All the hate and anger I had felt as a youngster toward those crackers back home, I used against these yellow mother-humpers over here. I felt no remorse, just one less fool I'd have to deal with. But this one night, a mortar round hit near me, probably a 120 mm. I remember going airborne and thinking to myself, 'That's your natural ass, Joe.' But at least you're headed in the right direction. That was in pitch- black nighttime. When I came to, it was dawn, and I didn't have a scratch on me, but I was in a sea of death, dismembered, burnt, charred bodies, hunks of flesh and bone and innards. You couldn't tell who was black, white, or yellow. It was all just blood and guts. The skin, hair, eyes, don't mean a damned thing to the Creator. The Creator sees from the inside out, from the soul. That's what we are, son, eternal souls."

Papa Joe took a sip of his vodka, relit his pipe, and continued. "From that day on, I've tried to look at life and people from the soul side. I call myself a soul disciple."

Wes was jamming in the background. *Johnny Griffin* on tenor, and they were stretching out. I was chilling and digesting Papa Joe's thoughts.

"Pops, that's some heavy stuff you just put down. I've never heard life put like that. You took me to church."

"Just something to give you a little perspective on the big picture. All you can do is be true to yourself and try to do the next right thing." As Joe said this, his eyes lit up, and he had a small smile on his tough-guy mug.

We listened to guitar players all afternoon and into the evening. *Wes, Grant Green, Pat Martino, Kenny Burrell*—the scene was mellow. We played some dominoes and sent Baby Sis out to get some pancit canton and lumpia. Before I realized it, curfew time had crept up on me. I split for my barrio pad with my dome full of wise man's words, wondering what Papa Joe really saw in the soul side of America that made him cash out and leave for good. Everything is everything.

CHAPTER 16

As Tyler predicted, the next few days were very routine. The kiddie cathouse was vacant, kids and Mamasan gone, although the pictures Denny and Rory had taken proved that at one time there were several young kids at the location. Big Mama Conception Ramos was still on the lam. We did, however, put a name to the little dead girl. She had been Lourdes Garcia. I hoped wherever her soul was, it was a better place than where her body was left.

We stayed on port and starboard duty. On my work days, I did routine mundane housekeeping stuff: expense reports, updating my various qualifications—basically just policing up my desk. On my days off, I put in a lot of time at the gym, and in the evenings, I acted as a bouncer at Nea's place, but nothing and nobody needed bouncing. The two deaths that we'd begun to investigate were still eating at me. The little girl I could see was clearly a cover- up, she was the victim of the greed and perversion of adults. Deep down, I felt her death needed some atonement, some payback. I had rolled Papa Joe's thoughts over in my mind, but to say "everything is everything" seemed to demean that little girl's life. I vowed to myself that if I ever caught up with the scumbag that killed her, I'd make sure his time on earth would be short and not too sweet.

Phil Goins was a whole different bag. He was a grown man who made his own bed and was now lying in it, six feet under. There was so much other shit that didn't add up, his dealing with the tech rep Zimmerman and the two tall hookers, the ducats his wife received, the small-caliber round to his dome, the pure China white up his turd cutter—it was all so pat that I feel like he was a fall guy for something real heavy. I tried to impress upon Morris, who I'm sure is a company man, that there was more to the Goins case. When our investigation was shut down, I knew that Goins' death was the tip of something big, really big.

The arrival of the USS Constellation has been pushed back by a couple of weeks. This meant that life would be super slow in Olongapo City, but when the Constellation did hit port, it was gonna be some full-tilt boogie. I had thought about talking to McMillan about Goins some more, but he had called Tyler, telling him about our conversation, to which Tyler informed him that the Goins case was closed, and he didn't have to tell me squat. Tyler's words to me were, "Ricky, you're becoming a real pain in the ass. Goins is still dead, and his case is still closed. I got a call from a Jack McMillan saying you were asking around about the case. I don't even want to hear about you asking this guy about the score of a Cubs game, *comprende*?"

"Aye, aye, Skip, but I didn't say that this was for an ongoing case. I was just curious about a couple of things, but he put my questions to rest."

"Good, then let's move forward. We got no need to look back. The lawyers at the JAG write the last chapters on these cases. Ricky, you're a good investigator and a tough customer, but you think too goddamn much. Just do your job and try to enjoy life some."

"Right on, Skip. I'm enjoying life, but it seems like nobody wants me to do my job."

"Our job is what our bosses say it is. It ain't a job, Rick, it's a mission."

"Yeah, I dig that whole scene, Skip, but this idle time has got my mind going into Oscar Tango mode."

"Well, Rick, put your mind on R&R, and take a seventy-two. I'll see you on Friday."

"My man, I knew there was something about your coal-mining ass I liked."

Tyler actually cracked a smile, and a little chuckle passed his lips. "Okay, Ricky, shove off."

That's just what I did. It was a Monday afternoon, I got Nea and we went up to her place in San Antonio and laid around the beach drinking rum and cokes, smoking some Lebanese Blond hash Romeo turned me on to, screwing our brains out. Talk about "fun in the sun." When I got back to work, it was Friday the 13th. Tyler was off that day, but I felt refreshed and ready for duty. The situation was normal until that evening. I was in the Nueva with Denny and Rory, and they were telling me about coming home from a shopping expedition and finding Denny's son, Peanuts, with two young hookers running around the house buck naked with *Peter Frampton* blasting on Denny's sound system. He was laughing about it now, but I know old D.B. busted a gasket when he took in that scene. "That goddamn boy's hung like a pony and got good taste in women, too," Denny crows.

"Like father, like son," Rory adds, laughing.

"All right y'all, you don't have to go biological on me. I get the picture," I say.

After another Jack, I bid Rory and Denny good night, light up a Kool, and split. That's when Friday the 13th caught up with me. As I walked out of Rory's and stepped to the sidewalk, I ran smack into one of the biggest burr-headed, tattooed-up jarheads I'd ever seen. He immediately started getting racial on me.

"Nigger, don't you know to move your black ass out the way when you see a white man on Gordon Street? Take your monkey ass back to your jungle," he says to me.

I hear everything he's saying, but everything is starting to move in slow motion. I can sense a small red light and a train whistle going off in the far distance.

"Hey, Ron, he ain't all nigger. He's some kind of mongrel, long-haired spic, a nigger-mixed spic. Now that definitely ain't human." Says his rail thin, six-foot two buddy. The few people on the sidewalk back off to give us some space. The Marine starts poking me in the chest with a huge forefinger.

"I'm talking to you, mutt. You look at me, boy, when I'm talking."

Before he can say any more, I grab his finger with my left hand, jerk it out of its socket, and pull him forward. I put my right hand on the back of his burr head and bring my knee up to his mug. I could feel the bones cracking on my knee. He fell backward, and blood flowed freely from his nose and mouth.

His skinny partner looked at me in wide-eyed terror. I dropped his ass with a kidney punch and a right cross to the side of his noggin. I was about to smash skinny's head into the outside wall of Rory's place when I was grabbed from behind. It was Denny.

"Whoa, Ricky, what the fuck man, you're about to piss your career away on these two shitheads. That big sumbitch better survive or your ass is grass, son."

As Denny was talking, I could vaguely hear him as the train whistle and red light were receding back into my subconscious. The shore patrol and AFP had arrived. They sent for some corpsmen to take Laurel and Hardy to the base hospital. I was arrested for assault and battery and possible manslaughter, if big boy buys the farm. After Denny and me ID'd ourselves, they agreed to let Denny take me to the brig at Subic. I was processed, and my badge and gun were confiscated. I spent the night in the drunk tank by myself. The next day, Tyler came to get me out.

"Look, Ricky, your goose was almost cooked. That big fella almost slipped into a coma. They managed to get him stabilized, but he might have brain damage."

"Skip, can I get my badge and roscoe back?"

"Rick, for now you're on administrative leave. Take the time to get yourself together. This situation will straighten itself out. Denny told me it was clear-cut self-defense on your part, but you need to cool off for a while. You've been wound up ever since Goins' body washed up."

"What's the real deal, Skip? Am I in or out?"

"Rick, the real deal is your body is a dangerous weapon. You put that big boy's lights out but good. It looks like you got a couple of witnesses backing up your self-defense story. Also, his skinny partner is admitting they braced you pretty hard."

"So, I'm out of work because two shit-for-brains hayseeds jumped me?"

"Rick, this matter has to go through the chain. Denny says those two clowns are some of the Nazi boys from Club Viking. Big boy had swastikas and iron crosses all over his body. But you're still an officer of the law, and you kicked those fellas' tails but good. It has to be adjudicated."

"Can I get some of my gear from the shop, and how should I check in?"

"You can check in by phone once a day. Needless to say, don't leave the Subic area."

"Hey, Skip, I got a lot of unused leave and sick days. How about giving me three weeks?"

"We'll see how your case goes, and then I'll work something out. Just keep in contact with me or Denny."

When we get back to HQ, I clean out my desk. The last thing I grab is a manila envelope from the photo lab. As I peek inside, I see the flicks Smitty took of the pipe Roberto's crew found in the Jungle.

CHAPTER 17

The first few days of my mandatory vacation were nerve-racking. I was on pins and needles, wondering if that shit-for-brains that tried to brace me was fucked for good or not. Nea gave me a lot of space, sensing I was uptight. She did, however, try to get me thinking straight.

"Ricky, this thing is in God's hands. You know, you just defend yourself. If the man dies, that is his fate. If he lives, maybe you learn the lesson that violence is not always the answer."

"Wow, everybody's philosophizing—you, Papa Joe, Al. I'm glad I got big ears so I can take all this knowledge in."

"Ricky, all I'm saying is the outcome is already made, so no need to sit here sick with worry. I never see you like this."

"Well, doll, I got to admit, I kinda scared myself. I reacted without thought. It was just when I felt his jaw crack on my knee that I pulled back. If I'd continued and drove through, his chin would have been in his brain and he would have been DOA."

"Okay, Rick, maybe you lucky this time. Now, why don't you take a walk or go on base. Just get out from under my feet for a while."

Nea's advice was good. That situation that I didn't start but had violently finished was out of my hands now. I'd been holed up for three days, just going to the back gate to phone in to Tyler at 1100 each day, I did need some air. I ate a fried mango for breakfast, showered, and kissed Nea on my way out to check in. After talking to Tyler, I spoke with Denny for a while.

"Good news, pard, an old redneck came to your rescue. Bugs came into HQ and corroborated your story. Said he saw the whole deal go down, recognized you as my partner, said those ol' boys looked to be itching for some shit, but they fucked up royally when they picked you out of the crowd. Said he saw Big Boy poking at you, he blinked, and then Godzilla was out cold on the sidewalk, and you were dropping that skinny spastic."

"Cool. I hope that shows this wasn't assault on my part. But what about that overgrown fuck in the hospital?"

"Once again, Baptiste, you got a horseshoe up your ass. Big Boy has a broken jaw and nose and dislocated finger. Nothing that can't be fixed, no brain damage, though he'll be eating through a straw for a while. Might even slim down some. I guess Tyler was waiting on the disposition of your trial to tell you."

"No word yet, huh?"

"Nothing, but you're going to be exonerated on this one. Even that scrawny hillbilly with Big Boy, whose name is Ronald Acton, by the way, says they were looking to fuck up a colored that night. They just had the misfortune of running into the Baby Brown Bomber."

"Denny, you made my day. Man, Nea's been telling me to let go and let God deal with this shit. Now I think I can."

"All right, Bubba. You take it slow and don't get any on you. I'll see you in a few."

"Later on, D.B., and thanks."

For the first time since that incident, I felt relaxed. I walked out of the back gate and stopped at a hole in the wall called the Iron Butterfly that featured hard-rock sounds of the Nam days. As I walked in, I could hear *Hendrix* singing, *"Yeah, sing a song, bro, if the sun refused to shine, I don't mind, I don't mind . . ."* It was 1130, and *If Six Was Nine*, was blasting. A few hippie Filipinos and some stantiondito heads are drinking San Miguels and toking reefer out back of the club. I get a brew, blow through a few squares, and kick back with the sixty's scene, P.I.-style. I was digging some hip tunes by *Creedence, Steppenwolf*, and the bar's namesake called *"In the Times of Our lives."* Hard rock is not usually my thing, but I can dig any good music and the pure D, hang-loose vibe of these sounds has matched my mood.

I left and headed back to our crib, but remembered Nea telling me to get some air, so I caught a tricycle going back into Olongapo instead. Along the way, I saw Smitty and his wife, who was now visibly big with child. I got out of the tricycle and walked over to greet them. They smiled upon seeing me and returned my hellos.

"Smitty told me about that little girl," Celi said.

"Yeah, it makes you wonder where God's at when you see stuff like that."

Smitty answers, "It's up to us to do our part here on earth, Rick. We got to put in more than we take out."

"I can dig that," I say.

"Look, Rick, we're going up to San Marcelino to work at a little school that some Irish monks have built for the barrio kids. Why don't you come with us?" Smitty asks.

Without giving it a second thought, I answer,

"That's a bet. Let's roll."

Celi claps her hands, her face beaming in a huge smile. Smitty is holding her hand and patting me on the back with his other one, saying, "Rick, this is going to be a great day."

We catch a Jeepney and take the half-hour ride to San Marcelino. There are a few Nipa Huts and small concrete-block buildings. As we get out of the Jeepney, it seems as if everyone knows Smitty and Celi. I'm also warmly greeted. We walk to a neat, square block structure of about nine hundred square feet, which houses a one-room school with about thirty bright-eyed and eager Filipino youngsters, from six to twelve years old. They're being taught arithmetic by a pasty-faced Irish monk. The kids rush to greet Celi and Smitty as we enter their classroom. They pat Celi's stomach and hug Smitty. The monk, Brother Paul, gets the kids back to their brand-new desks. Smitty introduces me to Brother Paul and the class.

"This is Mr. Baptiste. He's a police officer on the naval base at Subic.

The monk smiles and says, "We were just discussing John the Baptist yesterday. Now we have our own Baptiste. I'm honored, sir," he says, and extends his hand in a hearty shake.

"No, sir, it is my honor. What you are doing here is outstanding work,"

"Mr. Baptiste, there is more of God's work to be done. Smitty can fill you in," Brother Paul says with a grin.

Celi remains in the classroom as Smitty takes me out behind the schoolhouse to a huge mountain of cinder blocks.

"We're going to build a small rec center for the kids with ping-pong and pool tables, a basketball hoop, and a crafts center."

"And you need my Yankee ingenuity to get these blocks up that hill?"

"No, brother, we need your colored-folk muscle to hump these blocks up there."

"Right," I reply.

"Rick, we'll get a working party together. There's a group of older kids that hang out at that pop stand over there. I give them a couple pesos and we got us a crew."

As we approach the young guys, Smitty hollers, "I need me some workmen. Ten pesos each."

He's damn near bum-rushed. All fifteen boys

line up, and Smitty hands each a ten-peso bill. We head back to the pile of blocks and form a line that extends halfway up the small hill. The blocks are passed man-to-man until the pile is at the halfway point.

This effort has taken a couple of hours, and in the P.I. heat we're all wringing with sweat. My arms are burning. I hadn't humped that much by hand since I was a seaman apprentice on the Coral Sea.

Smitty blows a whistle. "Okay, fellas, let's take five."

Celi and two other women bring some pan de sals and pop colas for the boys, and a couple of San Miguel's for Smitty and me. We rest for about twenty minutes, and Smitty blows the whistle again and looks at me, grinning. "Let's see what you got left, old dude."

"I got plenty, youngblood. Let's get it on." We re-formed our line from the midway point to the top of the hill, where a patch of earth had been cleared and leveled for the new structure. Smitty told me some Seabees were going to lay the foundation for the rec center just as they'd done for the schoolhouse.

After a couple more hours, we'd moved the

blocks to the hilltop. The work was hard but gratifying. It felt good to be doing something positive—putting something back in—when you work on the slimy side of life sometimes everything about life starts to look slimy, and this hard work was soothing my soul. I'd been smelling something like BBQ for quite a while, and said to Smitty, "Man, I smells me some poke around this camp."

"Yeah, the women are roasting a pig to christen our rec center."

"Man, I need to thank you and Celi. This has been the best day I've had in a long while."

At about 1900, we had the blocks situated to Smitty's specs. I was exhausted, but happier than I'd been in years. As the sun set, we had a small barrio fiesta, with much singing, guitar playing and lots of dancing and smiling faces. We drank cold beer and enjoyed the succulent roast pig. Later, as we rode back to Barrio Barretto, I looked at Celi and Smitty and thought what a fine day this had been. We hugged as we went our separate ways. I got back to my crib, gave Nea a kiss, and washed up before sleeping the peaceful sleep of an honest, working man.

The next day, when I called in, Tyler relayed what Denny had already told me.

"Rick, the charges against you have been dropped. In fact, the JAG office wants to know if you want to press charges."

"No, Skip, let's just let this shit lie."

"Your call, Rick."

"Skip, I would still like to take the next two or three weeks off as leave. I'm starting to get my head together."

"Okay, Rick, we got the Connie coming into port in about a week, and I might need you. You can pick up your badge and roscoe anytime. Also, you got a letter here from an R. Romag in Manila."

"I'll be in tomorrow, and we can get squared away."

"Okay, Rick, see you mañana."

I was on cloud nine as I walked back to the hooch, where Nea and I drank some brew, smoked a little more of Romeo's Lebanese, and laid around in the Papasan chair listening to *Santana* all afternoon.

CHAPTER 18

I make it up to HQ for muster the next morning and am greeted with catcalls from my fellow agents.

"You a baaaaaad man. 'Float like a butterfly, sting like a bee,'" Denny crows.

"Rumble, young man, rumble," Octavio adds.

Even Tyler gets into the act, saying, "Welcome our new agent, Ricky 'The Dragon' Baptiste." His saying this meant that I was still part of the team. Tyler continues. "Ricky's going to take a couple more weeks' leave. Hopefully the Connie's time here will be quiet, and I won't need to recall him."

"What's the Connie's updated arrival Skip?" Collins asks.

The whole eight-man team is there: Collins and his partner White, another salt-and-pepper crew in their mid-thirties who are both heavy juicers, Octavio and Greevy, and two younger guys on their first MIS tour, Denny and I, and of course Tyler, our skipper.

"Connie should be in on August 27th, next Friday. There hasn't been much cash in Olongapo since the Connie's last port call, but all the con artists, hustlers, part-time hookers, and other scumbags are heading back to PO Town for a payday." Tyler says.

"Well, Skip, with them bird-farm boys coming down from Yokosuka, they'll be ready to blow off some steam. Denny says.

"That's what I'm saying, gents. This could be the Wild West or the summer of love. We have to be ready for any contingency," Tyler says.

"Skip, we know the drill," Greevy says.

"Okay, Greevy, I hear you, and I want to talk a little about Rick's situation. He's been cleared, and the charges dropped." A big cheer goes up among the men. "The dismissal was primarily due to some very credible witness testimony that corroborated Rick's story, but the situation should never have gotten to where it did. We have all been taught to subdue whenever possible. Now, in this case, there were two assailants, which is why the JAG cut Rick some slack. Plus, I don't think Captain Rosen cottoned to all those swastikas tattooed on that big guy and saw this for what it most likely was—a racially motivated attack," Tyler says.

"Yeah, Ricky motivated those two birds not to mess with any more soul brothers," White adds.

"The point is to remain detached and objective, do your job, and not become part of the crime scene. We're off port and starboard. It's all hands until the *Connie* leaves port," Tyler says as the meeting breaks up. He motions me into his office.

"I got your mail here, Rick," he says, handing me a small stack.

"Thanks, Skip, I appreciate you going to bat for me with those JAG boys and for granting my leave."

"Well, the JAG office wasn't a problem. As far as they were concerned, this was self-defense, cut-and-dried, but giving your fighting skills, the question of excessive force did come up. This is a new volunteer military, and there's no hot war so, our actions are going to be under a microscope. That's the lay of the land from now on, Rick. It's a new playing field."

"I see what you're saying, Skip, and thank you again for having my back."

"Rick, we're a unit here, and you're a key component. I recruited you, and as long as your actions are righteous, I'll back you to the hilt."

"My man," I say, giving him a pound.

I walk back to my desk to look through my mail. A statement from Navy Federal, the mortgage for a bungalow that I own and rent out in San Pedro, California. A letter from my brother, Rey, updating me on him and his family, and one from my sister, Mia, who is thirteen and already considering the Navy as a way to get into the medical field. She's way ahead of where I was at that age. I feel proud that she would ask for my advice. But I couldn't wholeheartedly recommend the Navy to any woman, let alone to my baby sister. There are limited opportunities for woman in the Navy, they can't even serve on board the ships. I'll suggest she look into OCS, or even the Naval Academy, which just started accepting women.

My last two letters were from Maria and Rolfie. Maria was enjoying a successful tour, playing in Singapore at the famous Raffles Bar. She enclosed a photo with her trio. She was, as always, a stone fox. Rolfie had sent a manila envelope. I open it, and in it is a short note, accompanied by a five-by-seven photo and a row of negatives. The photo is in color and it's of the subject I asked Rolfie to have tailed, with two Asians, in what appears to be a warehouse.

The subject and the other man are looking at a piece of electronic equipment. The other person in the picture is a beautiful, tall Asian woman. This one picture brings the Goins case into sharper focus. It's a big piece of the bigger puzzle. I opened this can of worms, and I guess it's my destiny to follow it through. I need to talk to Jack MacMillan again, but since he spoke to Tyler, he might blow me off; and if Tyler found out, he definitely wouldn't consider that righteous on my part. I put my mail in a folder and hail a Guerrero taxi to Boton Wharf, making mental notes to myself: get with KC at the photo lab; try to run down Jack MacMillan; go by the BOQ.... The cab pulls up to the Fleet Air Photo Lab in Cubi Point. The big repair ship, the USS Jason, is parked directly in front of the lab at the pier. I don't go through the front of the lab, as I want to keep a low profile. I go straight around back to KC's trailer and walk in on him working on a Hasselblad camera.

"Yo, amigo, you studying that camera mighty hard."

"L'il Capone, heard you busted up a couple of shit-kickers pretty good."

"KC, you know I still see red sometimes. When

that big shithead started to fuck with me, I got steamed, but once he put his big-assed mitts on me, I had to clean his clock."

"Man, you're still the same mean, nasty SOB I met back in 1964. If you wasn't so pretty, people would run and hide from your rotten ass."

"Yeah, man, there's some truth in that. Good thing I hang around with zoo-faced saints like yourself. Maybe the good lord will take a liking to me."

"Yeah, Capone, go fuck yourself."

"Look, man, all that brawl shit is over and done. I was completely cleared of any wrongdoing. But I need a solid."

"Shoot, shipmate, *mi casa es su casa.*"

"I need some eight-by-ten blowups from these negs." I show KC the five-by-seven and detail the area I need blown up. He lays the negs on a small light table and scrutinizes them with a loop.

"You know, Cap, this shit was shot with an Instamatic, probably the 500 model. The negs are half-assed sharp, this 126 film is shit. I'll have Manny take a look-see. Why don't you write up a ticket?"

"Man, this is strictly off the books. I need this done on the QT."

"I hear you, my man, ain't nothing but a thing, Cap. But dig, I'm still waiting to catch those half-pint hammers at Rolfie's joint."

"KC, we gonna make that Manila run most ricky ticky, so you best get that ninety-six-chit signed off."

"All right, Cap, I'm gonna hold you to your word. I'm having wet dreams with those midgets in starring roles."

"All right papa-san, I'm going to hook you up, but don't start crying if your old ass can't handle that action."

"If I can't, I'll die on the down stroke with a shit-eating grin on my grill."

We both laugh and give each other a soul handshake. I catch a bus back to the BOQ to plot my next moves. In my quarters, I begin to put this puzzle together. And I think I can make it fit. I have the crime, the motive, and the perp, that explains Goins' death. But I need to run a couple of details past Jack MacMillan to check my theory through. I know that finding him in a talkative mood might be tough, but at least I know where to find him. I go down the hall to some pay phones, drop a dime, and call Cubi Point CPO club and have Mac paged.

"MacMillan, here."

"Mac, Rick Baptiste. I know you talked to my boss, and this conversation is completely off the record. But I have a couple more questions."

"Baptiste, I don't know what your game is, but count me out. I got nothing for you. I'm a civilian. I'm sorry about Phil Goins, but I ain't in that shit."

I got a dial tone, and I knew that it was a done deal with Mac. I needed to regroup quick and get a Plan B. I had to do some cross-checking on my theory. That's when I called Denny.

"Hey, D.B., Ricky here. Let me ask you something about the Goins case."

"Damn, Ricky, you just set on getting your crank in a wringer, ain't you."

"Yeah, I know, man, but I just want to tie up the loose ends in my own head, so I can put it to rest."

"What do you need, Rick?"

"You got the name of anyone at VRC 45 that I could talk to?"

"Let me check my notes on that," Denny says, putting the phone down. After a couple of minutes, he gives me the name Le Croix.

"Seemed to be a straight shooter. Works over in AIMD, we did some time on the Shangri-la way back when."

"Thanks, D.B., remind me to make that next C&C a double."

"You can bet on that, pard," Denny says, hanging up.

I get in touch with Le Croix and set up a meet on Sunday at 1500 hours, just two days from now. Then I call KC at the photo lab to see if he can put the ricky ticky on those prints.

CHAPTER 19

On the USS Constellation, the crew was jonesing hard for some P.I. liberty. For the past three months, they'd been operating in the South China Sea, with a brief port call in Hong Kong. Then they went north for a large exercise off Korea, with a short two-day liberty in Pusan. Then, because of engineering problems, they ended up in dry dock in Yokosuka, Japan, for a month. With the exception of the short R&R in Korea, no real cheap throw-down liberty with two-dollar hookers and two-bit drinks were available in Hong Kong or Japan. There was nothing like a third-world port with plenty of poverty-stricken women to brighten up the spirits of a bunch of low-paid enlisted sailor boys.

In the CPO mess, MS2 Renda was due to rotate to Hawaii for shore duty when the Connie arrived in Subic Bay, so Johnson would become the LPO of the night shift. Dawson and Lewis had finished their ninety-day mess-crank stints, and two new, nonrated men took their places: Jimenez, a Chicano from El Paso, and Tarantola, a tough Italian kid from Brooklyn.

"Man, I'm ready for some LBFMs. I could

hardly afford a drink, let alone some tail up in Yokosuka. I saved my dough for some real liberty," Renda said.

"Japan's super cool. You white boys is just from L Sevensville, and them Jap hammers don't dig no squares. Us brothers go straight to Tokyo. Mugan's is the spot, Jack."

"Hey, Johnson, I got your square and your Tokyo hanging," Tarantola says, grabbing his crotch.

"Boot Camp, the only thing you got hanging is your ugly mug. I've gotten more pussy on a bad day, than you got since you crawled out your mama's hole," Johnson says.

"Look here, fellas. Fuck all this rankin' on each other. Fact is we're all getting tail any way we want in P.I. This is my last port call on this tub. I'm going straight to the package store, getting my canned heat, then I'm gonna get me the two of the finest dancers from the High Plains and have myself a baby-oil bonanza," Renda says.

"Man, I gots to see that Benny. You going to have to dish out big pesos for those High Plains broads," Johnson says.

"Yeah, I got $1,500 US, and I don't give a rat's ass if I blow the whole wad. It's 1976, and I've been in this yacht club since 1970. I'm living like a king on this liberty: Royal Hotel, fine dames, plenty of booze—the whole nine yards. Dig that."

"I can dig it, Benny. You done did your Haze Grey time. Hell, I'll party with you, even listen to that 'Freebird' shit," Johnson says as Jimenez, Tarantola and Renda laugh out loud.

The sense of anticipation is similar among the denizens of Olongapo. The big-time bands were back at Foxy Brown's and the High Plains. Many women had returned from their home villages and city slums, along with the pickpockets, dope dealers, Benny boys, and street kids—all geeked up to relieve some US squids of their greenbacks. It was situation normal, at last. At the 7th Heaven, a new band, the Brothermen, was working out their routine. This was a nine-piece group made of six sailors from the 7th Fleet band on horns, bass, and drums. A PR stationdito, Angel Colon, on percussions, and two Filipinos on guitar and keyboards. It was the brothers from the fleet band that turned this show out. The 7th Fleet band was based up in Yokosuka but traveled with the command ship *Oklahoma City*—the Okie Boat—and were in P.I. for a month of concerts. But on their off time, some of the guys took the show on the road. The three horns were super tight. They had the *J.B.'s, Kool & the Gang,* and *Tower of Power* down to a T. The leader and lead singer was Charlie Boy Adams from Macon, Georgia, who could flat-out sing his ass off. The group was going through some instrumental stuff by *Kool & the Gang, "Who'll Take the Weight," "Funky Stuff,"* and *"Hollywood Swinging."* They then slowed it down with *"Wichita Lineman,"* with Charlie Boy playing a second keyboard and various percussion instruments. The dancers, bar girls, and hookers had crowded the club just to hear the new supergroup and to work on the dance steps they'd seen on *Soul Train*, which aired on AFRTS. Baby Black was holding court.

"Listen to that music. It blow my mind. I'm going to fuck Charlie Boy brains out tonight. He with me from now on."

"Sister, you never talk like that. We here for money not music," says Lillie, another P.I. soul sister.

"There's never music like this in P.I.," Baby says.

"Well, that's more money for the rest of us,

cause USS Connie fat with GI money," Lillie says.

"Right on, Lil, you get yours, 'cause I got mines," Baby Black says, winking and waving to Charlie Boy, who looks like *Richard Roundtree* and sings like *David Ruffin*. Charlie Boy blows a kiss at Baby Black, thinking about how heavenly that big ass had been these past three nights. Almost like his main squeeze back in Georgia. But for Charlie Boy, there would never be any woman who could hold a candle next to a true-blue, born, bred, and cornbread-fed U.S. soul sister. It didn't matter how fine these Asian hammers were.

The band then launched into their signature tune, "*Still a Young Man*," Charlie Boy crooning, "*Down on my knees, heart in my hand, I was accused of being too young.*" The girls were screaming, the dancers were grinding it out on the floor, and it was clear that when the Connie hit port, Olongapo was going to pitch a stone bitch. This same scene was being played out at the other big joints, The High Plains and Foxy's. The stationditos getting a few nights of cheap P.I. liberty with the class A girls and bands before the fleet pulled in and fucked up their wet dreams. But at Papa Joe's Green

Dolphin, it was dark, cool, and mellow as ever. I was sipping my usual and smoking a Kool. Joe had a vodka tonic, and his pipe had that great-smelling cherry blend. In the background was *Miles Davis's "Relaxin',"* with *Trane, Philly Joe, and the Boys.*

"You know, Juney, I'll be glad to see that bird farm pull in here. This camp starts getting cannibalistic when the fleet's out."

"I can dig it. Too many parasites and no host."

"Yeah, that's it son."

"Pops, I think I got the angle on that Goins case, but I need to cross-check a couple of things. I'm starting to see the big picture, and it's real big."

"Juney, there's a lot of shit goes down that's foul over here. Plenty of heavy hitters running around. That case got closed quick for a reason, son. Shit's supposed to run downhill. You stickin' your nose where it don't belong might have it to run uphill, and that ain't cool."

"I'm running this one down. I'm sick of sweeping shit under rugs. Hell, I just fought a war on a BS tip and those fucking Russians got our shit anyway. I'm seeing this one through for my own peace of mind."

"Look here, son, you on your own. You a grown-ass man way past three times seven. It's your call. If your soul gets put on ice, I'll put some silver dollars on your eyes and play some *Louis* for your dead ass."

Joe and I drink our oil and dig on *Miles*, not saying much more.

CHAPTER 20

The excitement and anticipation of the carrier-group's arrival extended up to my doorstep. I left Papa Joe's before sunset and got to our crib in the Barretto just as the sun was going down. It was a beautiful red sky at night, a sailor's delight. When I walked into the crib, I saw a real sailor's delight, Nea was with Amy and Josie, two of her best-looking girls, who were both standing on small boxes as Nea was making adjustments to their skimpy go-go outfits.

"Damn, honey, what we got going on in here?"

The two girls laugh and pretend to cover themselves.

"Well, Ricky, Amy and Jo-Jo going to be dancing on the pier at Subic to welcome the Connie with the High Plains Number One Band."

"Well, if all you two are wearing are these little pieces of cloth, those squids manning the rail are going to jump overboard."

I walk over to my stereo and put some *Led Zeppelin* on. *"Whole Lotta Love"* is blasting the walls.

"Y'all might as well get used to this hard rock

'cause that's what Enrique and his boys play," I say. Amy and Jo-Jo start getting down in that wild white-boy freak style. I knew they would be smash hits with those flattop sailors.

"You see, Ricky, my ladies ready for Freddie."

"I can see that, Mamasan."

The girls danced through the song, then got back to business, with Nea putting the finishing touches on their outfits. I changed the sounds to some *Mongo Santamaria* and went out back for a smoke and a brew. The girls put on their street clothes and boogaloo-ed out the door to *"Watermelon Man."*

"Nea, those two are something else. I'm surprised they ain't married and back in the world already."

"Josie is getting married to an Italian guy on the Connie. He transferred from the Kitty Hawk to come back to P.I. for her."

"Well, I can't blame the cat. She's a bad little hammer, just like you, mamacita."

The next morning, I was awakened by the loud, full-throttled sound of a classic Indian motorcycle, and Nea hollering, "KC, you still loco loco. Ricky still sleeping."

"I ain't sleeping no more. That mickey ficky could wake up a dead man with that scooter."

"Yeah, well, wake your dead ass up, Cappy, I got those urgent photos you needed so bad. Hand-delivered by PHCS Kenny Carson Streeter. That's right, shipmate, you're looking at the newest Senior Chief Photo Mate in the USN," KC says, grinning.

"Right on, my man," I say, and give KC a high five, then draw back to tag him on the arm.

"Not so fast, sand crab. You ain't got the rank to tack shit on me. But I would be honored to have you and your lady at my promotion ceremony."

"That's a bet, senior. We'll be there with bell-bottoms on."

"Well, hasta la vista, y'all." KC hops back on the big chopper and thunders off toward town.

I open the packet and look at the blowups. There are three people: the white dude, who was the subject of my surveillance, and two Asians—a middle-aged guy in a dark suit, and a good-looking young woman wearing sunglasses. The two men were looking at a piece of electronic equipment. I show the picture to Nea and ask if she recognizes anyone. She doesn't, but remarks on how tall the woman appears to be.

"Do you think these two are Pinoy?" I ask as I point to the Asians.

"No. Face and body look Korean or Chinese. Kinda hard to tell with those sunglasses," Nea says.

"I think you might be right, doll. This whole deal could be from the People's Republic with love."

"Ricky, what the hell are you talking about?"

"Just a hunch, honey."

That Sunday I went by taxi to VRC 45 to speak with LeCroix. I was armed with the photos Rolfie had sent, along with the shots of the pipe that Roberto's men found. I walk up to the quarterdeck, ID myself, and ask where I can find LeCroix. The airdale on the watch points me to the AIMD shop. As I enter, I'm directed to an office in the rear of the large avionics- and electronics-filled space. The name LCDR Miller is on the door, along with that of AECS LeCroix. I knock and enter. A tall, slim white guy with gray hair and a trim mustache stands, and we shake hands. I introduce myself, "Senior Chief Ricardo Baptiste. Thank you for your time."

"What can I do for you, Baptiste?"

"Just a couple off-the-record questions relating to the case of AEI Goins. I've got a few photos here, and I wonder if you could ID any of the people or objects?"

"Okay, let's have a peek." As he's looking through the photos, he says, "I don't recognize any of these folks, but this instrumentation that the two gents are holding looks to be a radar-jamming receiver probe from a prowler."

"That's an EA6B?"

"Yeah, that's right. That radar jammer is only in the EA6B. Does this stuff have something to do with Goins' death?"

"Don't know, Senior, were any aircraft parts missing, or any unusual requisitions made while Goins and the tech reps were here?"

"None to my knowledge. We worked with a bird that was on loan from one of the Kitty Hawk's squadron out of Whidbey Island. Basically, just getting familiar with the bird's quirks and structure. Any ordering for our training was done by Zimmerman."

"That's my other question: Is the white guy in the picture Zimmerman?"

"No way. This guy is clean-cut, slim, with straight hair. Zimmerman was heavier, a little shorter, with bushy hair and a beard. Also, Zimmerman's hair was reddish, and he wore glasses. No way—this guy ain't even Zimmerman's cousin. But that chippie looks pretty long and tall—like they say Zimmerman's girl was—but I never saw her myself."

"Thanks, Senior, you cleared up a couple of things for me."

"You know, Baptiste, I know this case has been closed, but Denny called me and asked me to give you five. We go way back to the *Shangri-la* in 1959 and 1960. He said you were on the level."

"Well, Senior, you gave me lots of food for thought."

"Glad I could help you, Baptiste. Give Denny my regards," Le Croix says as we shake hands again, and I leave.

I've got a real clear picture of what went down, but it's way over my pay grade. The basics of a plan had been marinating in my mind for a while. Talking with Le Croix verified most of my suspicions, there was one missing link I needed to connect in the chain of Goins' murder. I would write a letter worded so the subject in question, my missing link, would know that I had the big picture and had also peeped his hole card. I knew why Goins was offed and who was responsible. I wanted Goins' name cleared and his family taken care of. I also needed an insurance policy in case I got bumped off. So, I would send a copy to my brother, Rey, in Jersey, with instructions to go to the newspapers with my story in the event of my death. As I composed this letter, the magnitude of what I'd stumbled onto was tripping me out. If my theory was in fact true, it called into question our country's actions since World War II, all through this long Cold War. I knew, from my own life as a black man in America, that half of everything that was claimed to be freedom, democracy, and opportunity was a front for greed, theft, and corruption.

Although I felt my analysis was plausible and probable, I had been so indoctrinated by Uncle Sam's Cold War propaganda that the implications of this case were hard for me to swallow. This was almost like two separate cases. First, there was the murder of Goins, which was for greed and personal gain, then there was the larger door that Goins' murder opened, which led to one place, and it was a place that seemed too off the wall to be true. But it is what it is, and I'm throwing it out there in this letter to see who takes the bait. I finish banging out the letter on my Smith-Corona. The next step is to ask Nea to retype it in triplicate on one of the old Royal typewriters from Esperanza's Secretarial School in Olongapo. Once these three letters are distributed, the ball will start rolling toward what will most likely be my untimely demise.

After drafting my letter, I head to Nea's Misty Blue Bar so I can run down my plan to her because she'll play a key role. Before I even say a word, Nea reminds me about the Connie's arrival.

"Ricky, you know the Connie is in port on Tuesday, and I'm in charge of having go-go girls at the pier to greet the ship."

"I know, honey, but I need you to do me a heavy solid."

"Okay, as long as I here on Tuesday."

"I got that Goins thing figured out, but I need you to do some typing for me and then make a run to Manila to post a letter from the Manila Hilton. Then go by my friend, Rolf Romag's club, and give him two words: *Rojo* and *Verde*. He'll know what's up. That's it, doll. Then I can get this monkey off my back."

"Ricky, what monkey? That case closed. Just turn the page."

"I wish I could, but this shit stinks beaucoup, and I'm the main cause of Goins being the fall guy. There's a big, slimy mess on this one, and I'm putting some light on it and clearing Goins' name."

"Okay, I hope you know what you're doing. I don't care about Goins, I care about you, and you poking around where you don't belong. What if you *pagpatay sa tad.*"

"With your help, that won't happen, and I'm gonna hook me a crook and a killer."

"I'll type your paper and go to Manila, but I need to be back on Monday, and I need to spend a night in the Hilton."

"Right, that's a yard a night. What do I look like, Rockefeller?"

"Hey, Big Spender, you want my time, get off that dime."

"That's some cold-blooded shit, doll, but I can play that tune," and I hand her $250 US in pesos.

"Ricky, you played me now. That's cold-blooded."

"Nea, I need you all the way through on this operation."

"Okay, I'll type your letters and hand-deliver them. I'm sick of living with you and Goins."

"Yeah, me, too. It takes a lot of energy to be restless, irritable, and discontent all the time."

Nea and I walk from her club toward the Victory Liner Station and Royal Hotel. Along the way are some restaurants and bars that cater to Filipinos. There are several trade schools, and many tailor and shoe shops. Esperanza's school is above a small beer garden. We go upstairs into a classroom with twenty vintage Royal typewriters on even older desks. I explain to Nea what we need to do, and after a little small talk, she gets down to typing. She's just as good a typist as she is a seamstress. I review her handiwork. It's perfect.

Nea gives me a perplexed and worried look, and says, "I hope you know what and who you're dealing with. This is way more than dead soul brother in Subic."

"Yeah, baby doll, this shit is real deep."

To expedite Nea's mission to Manila, I would need KC's help. After posting my two letters to my brother Rey—one for the Goins family inside a larger envelope, and one with directions for Rey—we left the base and headed to KC's crib on the east side of Olongapo City.

"Is there a Senior Chief Streeter in this hooch?" I yell through the screened door.

"Who the fuck needs to know?" comes the bearish reply.

"Man, it's your old shipmate, Ricardo, and watch your trap. I got my lady out here."

"Well, Cap, I'm getting me some trim in here, so why don't y'all scram and come back in an hour."

"KC, you a sixty-minute-man now? That's not what I hear," Nea says, laughing.

"Look, Cap, you and Mamasan ain't blowing my natural high, so beat it before I really get pissed off."

"Solid, I'll be back in a few, but this shit is important, so don't split till I get back."

"I'll be right here with my bells on," KC says. We can hear Mimi and Fifi giggling in the background.

"That KC is a dirty old man. He will never go back to the world, can't have two wives there," Nea says.

"Doll, never put anything past old KC, especially when women are involved."

We took a Jeepney back to our place and agree that if KC can take her to Manila on Sunday, she can carry out her business and be back by Monday with plenty of time to get ready for the Connie's arrival. Nea starts to pack an overnight bag and I head back to KC's hooch. Once again, I holler through the screened door. "Yo, yo, you old anchor clanker! Get up off your hind parts and give a fleet sailor a drink."

"Help yourself, swabby. You know where it's at."

I walk in, head to the kitchen, and grab a cold San Miguel from the fridge. KC saunters out in some cutoffs and flip-flops, with Mimi and Fifi both buck naked, rubbing his hairy belly and chest. Looking at this sight I have to laugh, thinking old KC is living every sailor's wet dream.

"You birds put something on your tails. I ain't sharing shit with Capone 'cept this cerveza."

The two run off laughing as I enjoy the sight of their round brown rumps.

"Now what the fuck, Cap, you messin' with my private time?"

"Motherfucker, please—all you got is private time. I need you to do me a solid," I say, and I run down how I need him to taxi Nea to Manila and back. I also remind him of the freaky-deaky midgets at Rolfie's place.

"Cap, that ain't nothing but a thing to do. Up Sunday, back Monday. No biggie. Tell Nea her chariot awaits."

"My man, I appreciate it."

After a few minutes, Mimi and Fifi split to go to the market wearing shorts, flip-flops, and tie-dyed blouses, looking like a couple of Berkeley coeds. KC and I drink a few brews and listen to his favorite album, the *Allman Brothers' At Fillmore East.*

"Hey, man, you seen Romeo or Jabbo lately?" I ask.

"Saw Romeo a couple of weeks back at his Pinoy Bar, said he was headed to Bangkok and

Hong Kong. That damn Romeo always got something cooking. I ain't seen Jabbo in at least six months."

"Well, all right, buddyro, 0900 tomorrow. Nea will be waiting at the crib." We shake hands.

As I head for the door, KC looks at the chunk of tinfoil that I slipped in his hand. "W-T-F-O," he says.

"From Romeo, to me, to you. Enjoy," I say, thinking that chunk of Lebanese is going to blow his military mind. Hope he can drive tomorrow. "KC don't take no more than a couple hits. This shit will definitely get you bent."

"Cap, everything is daijoubu."

I then walk to the Green Dolphin for a quick hook with Papa Joe, hoping to clear my head and kick back a little before I start this shitstorm. The joint is cool and dark as always. Joe is smoking a cigar. Baby Sis, Lettie, Starchild, and another young street girl are at one corner of the bar gabbing about the new band at the 7th Heaven and making plans for the Connie's arrival.

"Juney, what you know, good boy?" Joe asks as I walk in.

"Pops, I been working this Goins thing out, and I think I got the nitty-gritty. I'm putting myself in play."

"All right, now I done gave you my take. But it's your thing, son. Do what you gotta do."

"Pops, you know how I roll once my nose is open. I got to run shit down whichever way it flows."

"Like I told you, son, this ain't your fight."

"I'm making it my fight."

"Okay, Juney, I said my piece. Let me get that double Jack straight for you, rest your mind and dig on this *Horace Silvers Jody* grind, 'It's a Bad Side.' You know, I'll be happy when that bird farm finally pulls into Subic."

"Yeah, you and every Mamasan, thief, and hooker from here to Subic City," I say.

The cigar Joe is smoking smells great. I light a Kool, sip at my Jack, and dig the sounds. Eventually Joe starts talking about how blacks were excluded from almost all the government's programs designed to help the everyday folks—from VA bennies to FHA loans and Social Security. Most blacks were left out.

"Things finally started to open up in the sixties,

thanks to Martin Luther King, Miss Parks, Fannie Lou, Malcolm, and all them that fought that BS at home. I fought and killed overseas, paid taxes, and still didn't have no rights. I ain't living my life redlined as second class, and that's one thing I know, in the USA—if you black, you in the back. Believe that."

"Yeah, Pops, that's true enough. But I'm gonna make sure Goins' kids knew he was a stand-up guy, not a dopehead, and they're gonna get his government bennies. This shit is much bigger than Goins. It goes all the way up."

"That's why I'm telling you your ass can get dusted in a skinny minute, messing with those big boys, and you'll be just another dead spook who got too smart for his own good."

Joe put on *Horace Silver's Song for my Father* LP. I finished my drink, we hugged, and I split. The street ladies were still gabbing about sailor boys and Yankee dollars.

I got back to our place in the barrio, and Nea met me at the door in a transparent little black teddy that I'd never seen before. She handed me a Jack on ice. I took a long sip, digging the scenery in front of me, when Nea said, "Finish that drink, sailor, and TCB."

"Right on, *mamacita*."

We were still in bed when KC woke us, pounding on the door. "Get up, you horny lovebirds, it's time to drop this dime."

Nea jumped up and headed to the rain locker. I threw on some shorts, let KC in, and said, "Goddammit KC! I said 0900. It's not even 0700. Now *you* messin' with *my* private time."

"I wanted to be on time. That chunk of Lebanese got me all the way twisted. I figured I better get here early, before I get greedy and hit it again and really fuck up."

"My man, always right on time."

"We aim to please."

Nea walks out, looking bright-eyed and businesslike in a pants suit. "I look okay, honey?"

"Yeah, baby, gorgeous. I just hope Senior Chief here can keep his eyes on the road. Y'all on a mission."

"Mission impossible," Nea says as she winks at KC, and then gives me a long, lascivious kiss.

I grab her bag, throw it in the back of KC's Rover, and watch as they head off on the half-assed gravel road to Manila.

CHAPTER 21

Olongapo was revved up to a fever pitch. The Connie's much-anticipated arrival was less than forty-eight hours off, and this Sunday night is like a dress rehearsal. The town is once again crawling with hookers and their sidekicks, dope pushers, pickpockets, flower girls, beggars, and straight-up stick-up boys. Situation normal.

I decided to check out the 7th Heaven and see what all the commotion was about over the new supergroup, *The Brother Man Band.* As I walked on Rizal Street toward the Jungle, I started to realize how long I'd been going in and out of the P.I.—eleven years. I greet and am greeted by many shop owners, Jeepney drivers, kids, and hookers. There's a sense of relief in the air. The anticipation of the carrier group and thousands of horny, free-spending sailors have folks feeling good. I can hear and feel the band pumping and the joint jumping as I approach the stairs leading up to the club. As I walk upstairs, I hear some pumping horns blasting the *Tower of Power* hit *"You Got to Funkafize."* I can tell immediately that this band is right. As I enter, I'm surprised to see a packed house. Must be every stationdito brother from Subic and Cubi Point, and the five-hundred-man camp in this joint tonight, digging this new boss band and trying to cop some cheap tail before the carrier group arrives and the prices skyrocket. At the bar, I see Lettie, Baby Black, Starchild, and the rest of the Jungle crew. "San Miguel!" I holler to the bartender, handing him five pesos. The price in these clubs is three, and I tip him two. On the street, San Miguel goes for around fifty centavos. The clubs jack the prices way up, but it's still only about fifty cents US. The booze in most of these clubs is stone rot-gut, so San Miguel is all I deal with unless I'm at Papa Joe's. The squids and jarheads are drinking mojo and shake-em-up and other fruit-juice concoctions made with the cheapest vodka, gin, and rum in the 7th Fleet and guaranteed to send you on a slow ride into oblivion.

The Brother Man Band is smokin' in the spotlight on center stage. Fronting this group is Charles Z Addams — Charlie Boy — strutting, spinning, and gliding across the stage like Jackie Wilson. Charlie Boy was a complete fuck-up. He was a purple-shirt ABF on my last ship, the Ranger, back in 1972 and 1973 just before I went civilian. He was in and out of the brig and on restriction so often that all of us MAAs knew him by his first name. I'd heard him sing at a few clubs during some port calls when he wasn't on restriction, and found out he could play drums, piano, and arrange and write music. He'd been in the marching band at Grambling before he was drafted in 1970. He had a low lottery number, but somehow managed to enlist in the Navy. I arranged an audition for him with the Seventh Fleet Band, and now he's a dynamite attraction. I tip my brew to him and his boys. He catches my eye and salutes me as the band continues to groove.

"*Funkafize*" ends, and Charlie Boy says, "Thank you, ladies and GI's! This is *The Brother Man Band*, and we likes to get down deep into the funk. There's a brother here tonight who made this band happen. See, yours truly was fixing to do some serious brig time, and my man got me turned around and back to my music. Ya dig?"

The crowd whoops and hollers. One dude yells, "we can dig it, Charlie Boy!"

"That's him, Mr. Ricardo Baptiste over there. I call him the Latin soul brother. Give him a hand!"

I raise my brew and receive a hearty round of applause.

"Look, here, Rick, I know you digging this *Tower*, so we gonna run one down just for old times, and to get these dancers belly-rubbing. Let's hit it, fellas. *'Diamonds in the Sand.'*"

The tenor man picks up a flute and launches into a perfect rendition of one of the *Tower's* first and greatest hits. Charlie Boy is crooning, *"When God made you, he had a lot to do, in a day or two you were my dreams come true . . ."* The band was backing him exquisitely on this updated big-band love song. The dancers were grinding hard, and yelps and cries of approval came from all over the club. When the tune ended, Charlie Boy said, "Y'all, we got to take a pause for the cause, so dig on DJ Subway Joe for a few, and The Brother Man Band will be back for round two." DJ Subway lays on some *Blue Magic*, staying in the romance mood.

Charlie Boy walks over, pointing his big hands at me like six-shooters, and says, "Daddy-O, give your baby boy some."

We dap a short time, then he grabs me in a bear hug. He has an entourage of Baby Black and some of her girls and a couple bandmates.

Introductions are made, the percussionist, Angel Herrera, and I greet in Spanglish. He tells me he's from Ponce, I tell him my mom was from D.R.

"So, Rick, how you like our sound? I finally got me some cats that can play the way I hear shit in my head," Charlie says.

"Yeah, Charlie, you got something here. Y'all are tight, and you got this crowd uptight. But I'd like to hear these boys stretch out."

"I dig you, Rick, but these squids are here in Olongapo to party, not listen to none of my musical excursions, but I have worked out a boss instrumental arrangement of 'Cohelo' by *Mandrill*. Stretched it to twenty minutes or more. We'll run it down toward the end of the set."

"Right on, but that might be past my bedtime."

Baby Black asks if I need some company. I tell her I'm cool, but she has a slim, good-looking girl sit next to me anyway.

"You don't ask Mr. Ricky for nothing. Just sit there and look good for him," Baby Black says to the girl, whose name is Gloria.

"Hey, Rick, what's with the brew? Thought you liked it dark on ice," Charlie boy says.

"Man, I don't mess with that rot-gut they serve in these joints."

Charlie Boy calls the barkeep over and instructs, "Mr. Baptiste here drinks out of my shit with the good ice, *comprende parico*?"

The barman smiles and pulls out a tumbler, puts three cubes in it, and pours me a double Jack from a half-gallon bottle.

"See, Rick, I even learned to drink from you. You don't pay for shit up in this hooch—booze, or pussy. Ya dig?"

"I can dig it. Now go on and do your thing, young man."

The band returns to the stage and launches right into *Kool & the Gang's "Funky Stuff."* The crowd is all fired up and hollering, *"Shit! Goddamn! Get off your ass and jam!"* Charlie Boy was leading in call and response. He would holler, *"Say what?"* and the crowd would continue their chant: *"Shit! Goddamn! Get off your ass and jam!"* The Brother Man Band went right into some *Ohio Players* and *Average White Band* as the dance floor exploded in a fury of feet and legs and arms clad in platform shoes, denim, and polyester double knit. Gloria asked if I wanted to dance. I declined and gave her forty 'P' and told her to go have some fun, and to tell Baby Black I was okay. I had another Jack and dug the scene for another hour or so. As I was splitting the club, the band segued into *Mandrill's "Cohelo."*

I ducked out of the club, lit a Kool, and hopped in a Jeepney to the main gate. Over on Gordon Street, Denny B was in VP Alley drinking a 7 and 7, smoking a Lucky Strike, and shooting darts with Bugs.

"Bugs, I appreciate what you done for my youthful sidekick, Baptiste."

"Hell, D.B., I just told it like I saw it. I didn't realize the colored was your partner. I just saw those two hillbillies brace him. Blinked my eyes and they was on the ground, and you were holding your boy back from seriously pissing on their cornflakes."

"Well, I appreciate it all the same. How's it hanging otherwise, pard?" Denny takes a long pull of his 7 and 7 and a hit of his Lucky, while throwing another bull's-eye.

"Goddammit, D.B., I'll be glad to retire to get away from your dart-throwing ass. You been raining on my parade for at least twenty years now."

"Retire? What the hell are you talking about now, Bugs?"

"Yeah, shipmate, I'm hanging it up. We just got this spade—uh, colored, XO—and I can't make myself call this moolie 'Sir' and salute his black ass on a daily basis. Coloreds are all right in my Navy as cooks and stewards, even title less waves, but not as my XO or CO. This equal opportunity is horseshit."

"Bugs, I tried to tell you the world was changing, and we gotta change with it or life will pass us by."

"That's all right for your Canadian ass, but I'm from Pittsburgh, and we don't tolerate no jigaboos bossing us around. That's how I was brought up," Bugs says as he sips on his San Miguel and matches Denny's dartboard throw.

"Doggone, Bugs, you're getting better with age like a fine Muscatel."

"Yeah, fuck yourself, D.B. I'm 100 percent aged Irish whiskey, best of the best."

The two buddies drink, shoot darts, and talk about old times while listening to Bugsy's favorite singer, *Freddie Fender* croon, "*Before the Next Teardrop Falls.*" The bar was packed pretty tight with VP sailors and their steady

269

girls, all knowing that the carrier group's arrival would mean the end of this laid-back period of low crime and cheap tail. Many of the women would hook up with the fleeties for some quick cash, leaving their boyfriends drinking alone and pulling their dicks. Mumbles was holding court to nobody in particular, while winking at Denny and licking her gums.

"Hey, D.B., it looks like MacArthur's mama wants your Tomahawk," Bugsy says.

"Man, that old bird is an instant soft-on."

"Better you than me, shipmate."

"Bugs, why did you get a new XO in the first place?"

"The old one, Big Daddy Schultz, all of a sudden got orders up to Maine, and was gone just like that, and this colored LCDR Holmes took his spot and man, I'm through. A spade XO is too much integration for me."

"Bugs, you're full of shit, but that's on you. By the way, what did this Big Daddy Schultz look like?"

"'Bout six one, trim, fit, and AJ squared-away, bald as an eagle. Hell, the troops called him 'watertight,' but the SOB had a Navy Cross and some other heavy fruit salad. He was one snooty bastard, always by the book, never got to know the men, didn't smoke, and hardly drank. A real stick-in-the-mud."

"Yeah, when did he transfer?"

"About a month ago."

"That so?"

"That's a fact, Jack, and I'm transferring to CIV Fleet, going up to Idaho. I won't have to deal with any spades there. You can keep your minorities, D.B., it ain't for me."

"Bugs, you don't got to convince me, but I still think you're full of it."

The two continued to drink and shoot darts until last call at 2330. Bugs headed back to Cubi Point, and Denny walked across Gordon Street to Rory's crib, which was above her club.

CHAPTER 22

KC dropped Nea off at my quarters on Cubi Point at around 1500 on Monday. She gave me a debrief on her mission to Manila, which went off without a hitch.

"I did just what you asked, Ricky, posted the letters at the Hilton, went out for dinner and then dropped by the Daktari Club to give your friend the code words."

"That's good, doll. Now, how did you and KC hook up?

"He met me in the Hilton Lobby. We had breakfast, then caught a cab to the Bayview where he stayed, got his Rover, and headed back to Subic. KC kept talking about some little Indonesian women. I think he's in love."

"Yeah, I had Rolfie hook him up with these two midget freaks. I thought they might hit it off."

"Well, KC's stone in love. Maybe Mimi and Fifi get walking papers soon."

"I don't think so, doll, KC's real loyal and damn horny. He might try to get all four of those birds at his pad. He was always a greedy man."

"All you sailors' greedy men. You, too, Ricardo. You want your cake and your pie, too."

"Now, you know baby, I'm merely a young man trying to make a way for myself in this mean old world. I want to thank you for running this errand for me, if this dude I'm hunting is who I think he is, and he tracks this letter, he'll run into a brick wall. I just hope he takes the bait."

"Ricky, these guys are smart and powerful. Why would they take your bait?"

"Because I think the cat I'm after is dirty, and he's running his own game on the side. I'm betting he doesn't want his bosses to peep his action. He'll want to meet me just to put me on ice or pay me off to keep my trap shut."

"Ricky, that's what scares me. If these guys want you gone, you disappear."

"That's the real deal, doll, but you ain't never seen me back down from nothing or nobody, and I ain't starting now. Besides, I got some heavy hitters on my side too. That's why Goins' name's going to get cleared, and I'm walking away on my own two."

"I hope you're right, Ricky." Nea reminds me about the Connie's arrival and her need to make sure her dancers are squared away. She showers, puts on a sundress, and we walk to the Sampaguita restaurant on Cubi Point for a nice dinner. Afterward, we catch a taxi to the main gate. I walk her to her club, the *Misty Blue*, have a beer, and listen to *"Fly, Robin, Fly"* and some of the other candy-assed disco music she plays there. The only customer is a young CB who's in love with Amy. I finished up my brew and split, telling Nea I'd be at the barrio pad and would escort her and her dancers on base the next day for the big bird farm's arrival. As I left the Misty, I thought about checking out the Green Dolphin, but I didn't feel much like talking, not even with Papa Joe. The actions I'd just taken with Nea's help had lit a match, but that small flame could become a raging fire. The question was, could I control what I'd just ignited?

I caught a tricycle out to Barrio Barretto. The driver was about fifteen or sixteen, and talkative, wanting to know all about "the world" and how he could join the US Navy. This kid had enthusiasm and obvious intelligence. He was short, scrawny, had bad teeth, and an even worse complexion, but I could feel this kid had plenty of heart inside his skinny-assed frame. He said his name was Javier Gomez. When we got to my crib, I gave him twenty 'P' and my card. Told him to get his birth certificate and keep in touch, and that I would see what I could do. Javier thanked me profusely and drove off, looking like he'd hit the exacta at Hollywood Park. Many of the kids I meet want to join the Navy and go to CONUS. I had helped a couple who were Nea's cousins, but this kid caught me at the right moment, and his English blew me away—perfect SoCal surfer.

The next morning, Nea and I woke up early, had our coffee and cigarettes, took a P.I. shower, dressed, and headed out to get Jo-Jo and Amy. The girls lived near the Victory Liner Station, where they shared a room. I had a hot pan de sol and a cola, while Nea rounded up her crew. As I savored my P.I. version of an empanada, all three came out laughing and smiling. Jo-Jo and Amy looking all "plain Jane" in blue jeans, cotton blouses, and flip-flops. Nea was wearing a powder blue pants suit and white platform heels.

"Hi, Mr. Ricky, you going to chaperone for us?" Amy asks.

"No, ladies, that's Nea's gig. I'm just your escort to the base."

We hail an empty Jeepney and take the short

drive to the main gate of the naval base. We pick up three other passengers along the way: a couple Filipino shipyard workers and a stationdito squid looking like he was still fried from the previous night's activities. We got out and walked across the Shit River footbridge. Then had to go through security to enter the base. I flashed my badge and walked the women through, no questions asked. One of the AFPs on the gate was a buddy of mine from the *Ranger*. He took a long look at the three bad hammers I was with and said, "What, you Iceberg Slim now, Ricky?"

"Look here man, I'm just taking these ladies out to the pier so they can properly greet CV64. This is my lady, Nea." I introduce him to the women.

"Well, carry on, my brother, you damn sure looking good."

"Right on man, I'll check you on the rebound."

"Dig it. I'll be right here."

We walk past the Money Exchange, and right to the pier where the Connie will tie up. Subic Bay is a beautiful deep-water port. It can handle a couple of bird farms and many smaller ships. The sun is just over the horizon, and the pier is a mass of activity; trucks, forklifts, vans, cranes, and all types of sailors and dockworkers. There's a stage that was rigged by the Seabees, and the High Plains Number One Band is getting their gear set up on it. The lead guitarist, Enrique Paz, was standing in front of a bank of Marshall amps riffing on a Red Gibson, sounding just like Santana. There were six small platforms in front of the bandstand, each about four feet high. These were for the go-go dancers. It was around 0700. The *Connie* was a couple of hours away from tying up. Nea and Enrique were talking and pointing at the small platform. Nea walks over to me, saying, "Ricky, I got to get my ladies together. There are four other girls from the High Plains I need to round up."

"Okeydoke, I ain't going no place."

There are several tugs in the harbor ready to assist the USS Constellation into its slip at the pier. At a little past 0800, the band is cranking through its hit parade of *Frampton, Skynyrd, Grand Funk Railroad*, and other hard-rock acts played to perfection by Enrique and his boys. Nea escorts the dancers out, and they all have red, white, or blue robes on and carry red, white, or blue platform heels. Once the girls get on their small platforms, they drop their robes, revealing tiny bikinis with the stars and stripes pattern, kind of like Wonder Woman. It was definitely a sailor's wet dream. They danced through a couple of tunes, then sat down and lit up smokes, awaiting the big ship's arrival.

At 0845 the flattop and Skyscraper Island bearing the number 64 came into clear view, dominating the bay. Part of the crew was manning the rail in their tropical whites, but instead of the traditional Dixie-cup covers, these enlistees had knock off CPO lids. It looked like a convention of Good Humor ice cream men. As the tugs slowly guided the floating airport into place, the band and dancers got more hyped. Finally, at 1000, the fore and after brows were in place, and the one MC on board announced, "Liberty call, liberty call." The squids rushed down the after brow like convicts running out of San Quentin. Many of them had been eyeballing and waving at the dancers while manning the rail. Now, as they left the ship, they saw up close six tan-skinned, big-legged beauties, dancing to "*Layla*," being played by a Filipino guitar ace. It was a sun-drenched day, already eighty degrees.

As I took in this wild scene, I thought, Man, I'm glad I ain't working tonight. The sailors were a cross section of young working-class Americans. The brothers are slick in their double knits and platform shoes, the white boys in Levi's and T-shirts, and a bunch of dudes in between. Many were gathered around the dancers' platforms throwing money and hollering their approval. Jo-Jo was the obvious crowd-pleaser, and many dollar bills adorned her platform. Her bikini could barely contain her large breasts, which were rare in P.I., and the squids were going stone ape-shit as her sweat-glistened body bounced on her platform. The sailors were calling out their unique terms of endearment to her: "I love you, no shit. I buy you Corvette." Or "Marry me for ten days." The other girls were doing fine, too, but no one grabbed the crowd like Jo-Jo.

There was a larger-than-usual AFP contingent to keep the throng in check. I found Nea off to the side of the bandstand looking at her girls and the sailors with a serious expression on her face.

"Rick, these GI blow all their cash on the pier. Look at Jo-Jo, she knee-deep in dollar bills."

"Yeah, these dudes act like they never seen any

tail before, but Jo-Jo is a stone hit. You might lose her to the High Plains."

"No way. Jo-Jo is in love with this big Italian guy. They going to get married and move to San Diego."

"Right on, but she's got a hell of a future in front of her on the go-go scene."

"She's got a nice future behind her, too," Nea says, pointing at Jo-Jo's tight round tail.

It was all over by noon. The band was packed up, the go-go girls were gone, and the Seabees were dismantling the stage. Nea had passed out over a hundred flyers for her club, Jo-Jo had collected over two hundred US, and Amy made close to a hundred. Nea and Amy headed back to the Misty Blue. Jo-Jo stayed behind to wait for her Italian honey, who'd cross-decked to the Connie to be with her. I went to the FRA and grabbed a chili dog and a something to wash it down. I figured I'd check on Nea and then head out to the Barretto.

By the time I left the base, close to five thousand wound-up and ready-to-blow-off-steam sailors had made their way across the Shit River Bridge and into Disneyland Far East. Most of these squids had a good month and a half of Yankee greenbacks in their pockets. Magsaysay was rolling from Gordon Street to Rizal. It was a banner day for all grifters. The Bonka Boat Queens and baby-boy divers were making many pesos from the sailors before they even got into Olongapo proper. Once on the main drag, the hookers were talking their talk; "Short time ten peso." "Best blow job in P.I., fifteen peso." "GI, I love you. No shit, buy me air-conditioned helicopter," and on and on. The kiddie pickpockets were running their game, along with the club barkers and dope boys. Vietnam and the sixties had been over for a while. The seventies still didn't have its own identity, but it seemed as if everyone in America was burnt out on all the heavy shit of the past ten years. People just wanted to kick back and party hard and P.I. was the ultimate place to party all the way down. Walking to the Misty Blue, I reflected on how much had changed since 1964, when I first hit Olongapo City. There was no draft or war, and the sailors today were more like cops or firemen, who changed into civvies to hit the beach.

I finally reached Nea's club, which was down near the end of Magsaysay, next to the High Plains. The street was jam-packed with the liberty hounds from the battle group. On the way, I ran into Jackson outside the duckpin alley acting as a junior pimp.

"Hey, GI, I got many cherry girl, twenty peso." He sees me and hollers, "What it is, Mr. Ricky."

"It's all you, Jackson. What the hell you into now? Look here son, don't let your business and my business cross paths 'cause I'd hate to lock up a little kid."

"Mr. Ricky, I try to keep nose clean, but these GI's got too many peso."

"You just watch your ass, there's some loco mother-jumpers out here today."

As I walk into the Misty, it's all I can do to squeeze through the doorway. The club is wall-to-wall sailors. Looks like Nea's ad campaign worked. I reached the bar and saw Nea mixing drinks and popping beer caps like an eight-armed whirling dervish.

She looks at me and says, "Ricky, don't just stand there with your thumb up your ass. Help a working woman."

"Aye, aye, Skipper. What and where?"

"You get beer. I mix booze. Okay?"

"Right on, mamacita."

Nea had brought five girls from her hometown, who, along with some freelance hookers and her regular girls made the Misty Blue standing room only. Some were waitressing in hot pants, tube tops, and tennis shoes, while the others joined Nea and me behind the bar.

"Mr. Ricky! Six San Miguel!" one girl hollers.

"Two seven-and-sevens, doubles!" Hollers another.

"Dalawong pitcher mojo!" another hollered.

It went on like this 'til around 1700, when the big bands at the High Plains, Foxy's, and 7th Heaven started to crank it up, and the drunk squids started to ramble down the main drag with their newfound brown honeys. The bar remained full, but manageable. An older sailor coughed up fifty US dollars for one bar fine. "I told Papasan fifty US, and he didn't blink. Pulled out a roll and peel President Grant right off," Nea said, somewhat bemused.

"These fleeties are flush with dough and got plenty of steam ready to blow. Might as well make hay while the sun shines," I say.

"I made enough hay today to start a horse farm. When GI's start drinking, they throw money away. Tomorrow they be broke asses."

"Yeah, but Friday's payday, and these fools ain't begun to party yet."

As the evening wore on, the crowd thinned out even more. A couple more-big bar fines were paid. These, Nea split fifty-fifty with her girls. I left, telling Nea I was going to Papa Joe's place, but I'd be back to pick her up at curfew. As I walk to the Green Dolphin, the cool air and sounds of *Esther Phillips* singing *"Home Is Where the Hatred Is"* greet me like a straight shot of pure D mellow.

"All right, Juney, we got your hook ready," Papa Joe says as he puts a tumbler of Jack on the rocks in front of me.

"*Esther Phillips*. Man, I used to dig her at the Parisian Room on La Brea back in LA, and she looked like she'd been down that junkie road."

"I can dig it, son, but I saw her in 1949 or 1950 with *Johnny Otis*. That hammer was built like a brick house with pipes from God."

"Yeah, she still had some bad curves in 1970 when I caught her."

Pops pulled off *Esther* after that one song and put on some *Lou Donaldson*. We jawboned about how PO Town jumped to life with this carrier visit. Hard to imagine that just a few years back there would have been up to three battle groups in port. Then Joe hands me an envelope.

"Your boy, Romeo sent a fellow around here to give you this letter."

I open it up and it reads: "Hey Cappy, I'm in Hong Kong for a while, but you know I got your back. Your Vato, Romeo."

"Thanks, Pops. It's not what I wanted to hear, but it's good to know the homes is still on this side of the dirt."

"Look, Juney, that's a fella who's gonna live to be old and ripe. When the Creator makes some mickey fickeys, he makes them to last. Can't kill 'em. Damn near like they go when they good and ready to go, and your boy is one of them MFs."

"Yeah, you right on that one, Pops," I say, thinking Papa Joe should know since he was one of those MFs himself.

I got Nea just before curfew, and we made our way to our crib by Jeepney. Man, it had been one long-ass day.

CHAPTER 23

I woke before the roosters the next morning. Something was bugging me, I didn't sleep well. There was a wild hair scratching at my brain. In the predawn hours it hit me, Romeo's letter was BS, first off. It couldn't have reached me from Hong Kong that fast, and second, Romeo never wrote in print. He had a perfect cursive script. This most likely meant one of two things; either the letter was total bullshit, or Romeo dictated it by phone to whoever told him I was looking for his thug ass. I hoped it was the latter, but Romeo or not, I was all-in. If Goins' killer showed himself, I was going to deal with him, with or without Romeo and his crew at my back.

Right now, the cards were up in the air, but they would hit the deck soon and I'd play out my hand. I boiled some water for some instant Joe and sat out back of the hooch, lit up a Kool, and watched the sun come up over Subic Bay. As Denny B would say, another fine Navy day was about to unfold.

Nea got up around 0700, fixed her coffee, and lit up on her Parliament. She came out back to sit with me. We both enjoyed the sunrise, absorbed in our own thoughts, not saying a word. I sat there thinking that if there was paradise on earth, P.I. could be the place; beautiful, lush land, pleasant weather, peaceful people, and gorgeous women. The only thing fucking it up was us Yankees with our arrogance, greed, and lust. Some MF's always got to have more. That's why even here in heaven there was dope, kiddie sex, and murder. It reminded me of *James Brown's* song, *"It's a Man's World." Brown* sings about all the wonderful things man makes, but above all else, man makes money. I knew money was at the bottom of Goins' getting knocked off.

Nea looks over at me and says, "What do you think on so hard? You look like a skinny, brown Buddha."

"I was thinking how beautiful the P.I. is and how Americans are fucking it up with our greedy-assed bullshit and arrogance."

"It's Americans now, but before Yankee it's Spaniard, before them, the Chinese, before that, Malay. All people arrogant and greedy. Yankee seem more so because they got so much already."

"You're on the real side of that, doll. I wish I had your brain. You can cut straight to the chase, I go up and down every street and alley.

Maybe you should do my gig, and I'll run the club."

"No way, honey. I get too jealous of you with all those girls."

"Yeah, well, the thought of you with a bunch of salty-assed sand crabs don't grab me either."

Nea makes us some more coffee. As she walks back out with the mud, she says, "I got to get to the club early to clean up. We made beaucoup peso yesterday. Me, Amy, and your little partner, Jackson, are going to start cleaning at nine o'clock."

"That's cool. You need an extra hand?"

"No, you just think Butch, that's what you're good at." Nea quotes a line from *Butch Cassidy and the Sundance Kid*, one of our favorite flicks. We both laugh and finish our coffee and smokes. Nea showers, dresses, and splits, giving me a kiss on my forehead.

It's about 0830, and Barrio Barretto is awake; the sound of Jeepneys and tricycles is in the air, along with the smell of various foods cooking. Mixed in are the voices of kids going to school and grown folks headed to work. Just another day in P.I. I got to wondering what type of damage the Connie boys did yesterday and decided to go by HQ and check on Olongapo's status from a police perspective.

After I did my shit, shower, and shave routine, I put on my khakis and a dark-blue guayabera, which, along with my CPO khakis and leather Puma running shoes, was my P.I. uniform. I made my way to the main gate by Jeepney. The mercury was already hitting eighty, and Ville looked no worse for wear. In fact, it looked even more alive and vibrant than usual. The bar owners and merchants were washing down the sidewalks in front of their establishments and the bar girls, looking like teenaged kids, were going about their business and running their games. Many sailors were walking around looking dazed and confused.

I walked on base and grabbed a pan de sol and a Coke on my way to HQ. As I walked in, I was greeted by Virgie, one of our middle-aged Filipina secretaries. I sat at my desk eating my breakfast. All the guys in my division were out except Tyler and Octavio, who were in Tyler's office. They hadn't noticed me yet. I finished my nosh and lit up a smoke.

That's when Tyler hollered, "Ricardo, WTF? I thought you needed some mental-health time?"

"I do, Skip, but I wanted to find out what kind of damage these fleeties did to the Ville yesterday."

"Minimal. These sailors ain't what they used to be. They're too busy looking cute and buying that five-dollar tail to fight and raise hell. I guess the best thing the Navy did was to let those birds wear civvies."

"Yeah, Skip, but it put a bunch of locker clubs out of business."

"Rick, those cats just got into another line of work, because wherever there are GIs, there's dough to be had. Bet your bippy on that."

"So, no rough stuff last night?"

"No, but the High Plains and 7th Heaven were packed way over capacity. We're going to have Shore Patrol limit the crowds for fire safety. Scuttlebutt is that the Connie's going to need some dry-dock work before she heads back to the CONUS, might be in Subic for three more weeks. You may end up getting your hands dirty when you come back in a couple of weeks."

"Skip, I got three more weeks, and I'm using every minute."

"Okay, Rick. Thought I could lasso you back a

little early. A month with these bird-farm boys could get dicey, especially when their cash starts to run low."

"You know where I'm at."

"Right, Rick. I'll call if we need backup."

I leave HQ and head to my base quarters, figuring to grab a run and pump some iron. After my workout I catch some z's, get up at 1600, shower, dress, and head for PO Town. I wanted to check the 7th Heaven and High Plains for myself. My first stop, however, was the Misty Blue. Nea's joint is full, but not like it was yesterday. Amy, Teo, and the regular girls are there, along with Jo-Jo and her sailor boy. As I walk in, Jo-Jo runs over to me, gives me a hug, and drags me to meet her fella—a big, burly Italian-looking cat.

"Honey, this is my uncle Ricky, Nea steady boyfriend. Rick, this my fiancé, Mikey," Jo-Jo says by way of introduction.

The big man stands at six foot three, 250 pounds. He's got me by four inches and fifty pounds. He extends a big bear paw of a hand, saying, "Michael Peter Tarantola, honored to meet you, Sir. Jo-Jo talks about you and Nea all the time. Man, you look more Puerto Rican than black."

"My mom's was Dominican, and my pop's is black American."

"Kinda like Reggie Jackson," Mikey says.

"Yeah, you could say that. I've been called a heavy hitter before," I say, laughing.

Mikey and I shake hands, and I wish him and Jo-Jo all the best. I motion to Nea to bring the two lovebirds a round. As they raise their drinks to thank me, I can see the happiness and pride in the big man's eyes as he looks at Jo-Jo, whose own eyes have that bright sparkle of a woman in love. I know that this is for real, not just a P.I. liberty hookup. I walk over to them and say, "Mikey, you got a great lady there. Treat her right."

"Sir, I love Jo-Jo 100 percent. You don't have to worry about me. I'm making Jo-Jo and the Navy my life. We're going to have a bunch of kids and live in San Diego."

"Yeah, I believe y'all will do just that," I say, shaking his hand again and hugging Jo-Jo.

As I walk back to the bar, Nea asks, "What you think of Jo-Jo's guy?"

"I think he's squared away, and they damn

sure in love.

"I think they will grow old together," Nea says.

And although we couldn't know the future, that's exactly what happened. They were true soul mates.

I nursed my drink and told Nea I was going to check out the High Plains and 7th Heaven. The High Plains was two doors down the drag from the Misty Blue, but in size and scope it was in a whole different planet. As I walked upstairs to the club, the sound of Enrique's guitar and those Marshall amps just about knocked me over. Enrique was deep into a *Led Zeppelin* groove, *"Living Loving Maid,"* and the joint was rocking at full tilt. It was 1800, and the bikini-clad go-go dancers were in their cages—shaking, strutting, and bustin' loose, drenched in sweat - their fine bodies glistening. The waitresses in their black mini cocktail dresses were damn near running to keep up with the orders. The band was jamming, and the mostly white-boy sailors were getting off. This was the biggest and most profitable club on Magsaysay Boulevard. It had air conditioning, the best-looking go-go girls and waitresses, and P.I.'s number one rock band. Enrique and his mates won the big Manila Battles of the Bands on a regular basis. I made my way to the bar, ordered a San Miguel, and took in the scene. As with Nea's place, the High Plains was full, but not packed, though it was still early. Enrique and the band started playing something I'd heard on AFRTS a few times called *"Do You Feel Like We Do."* The crowd was on its feet, singing along and lighting their Zippos in outstretched arms. Man, these squids were ready to party. If the High Plains was like this, the brothers over at the 7th Heaven must be turning that cabin all the way out.

Once again, the sound of the band knocked me back on my heels as I entered the club. *Earth, Wind & Fire's "Shining Star"* was wailing. It looked like *Soul Train* live: double knits, platform shoes, afros, free-form funky dancing, cigarette smoke, and plenty of oil being drunk. This joint was packed. Then Charlie Boy started the club chant:

"Shit, goddamn, git off your ass and jam."

"Say what?"

"Shit, goddamn, git off your ass and jam."

By this time a *Soul Train*–type gauntlet had formed, and the dancers were boogaloo'n down the line. The band kept the steam pumping going into a *Kool & The Gang* medley, and finally into *Sly Stone's anthem, "I Want to Take You Higher."* The crowd was at fever pitch when Charlie Boy slowed it up, saying, "Yo, looka here, this here is a Moog Synthesizer, and the only one in the P.I. Now, kick it while me and the fellas give y'all some summer madness." The band then rolled into a mellow hit by *Kool & The Gang.* I caught Charlie Boy's eye and pointed to him. He saluted me in return. As I split, squeezing back through the crowded dance floor, I saw Baby Sis with a short, clean-cut, brown-skinned kid hugging uptight. She saw me and smiled.

I walked over to Papa Joe's and, as always, the jazz was cool, and the joint was mellow. *The Crusader's* version of *"Eleanor Rigby"* was on the system. Pops put a tumbler of Jack on the rocks in front of me. There were a couple old-salt regulars with a couple older hookers playing Bid Whist at a table, and just a handful of other guys at the bar. Joe was talking about taking Big Red and another bird up to Angeles City for some big-money fights. I sipped my Jack and dug the sounds. One drink was it for me, I left Joe's at about 2100 and went back by

Nea's to tell her I was headed to the crib. Things settled into status quo almost like Nam times. This town could rise and fall according to the needs of the fleet and the people's need of Yankee cash.

I heard nothing of my scheme until a week after the Connie arrived. Then one day, Jackson came to my door with a message to go to KC's crib. When I got there, KC opened the door and said one word: "Verde."

CHAPTER 24

I'd come up with a convoluted arrangement of messengers and drops to eventually have the GO or NO GO on my plan arrive at KC's crib. When I got there, he handed me a small green envelope, inside of which was a small card instructing me to be at the Daktari in Manila at 1600 hours, on Thursday for further directions. That was about twenty-eight hours from now. This card told me I'd run this case down correctly and that my suspect had knocked Goins off because he got in the way of the skimming and back-door dealing from the scheme that was being run—a scheme so big it had to have Uncle Sam's blessing. There was no turning back now. I had to assume my suspect figured out who I was and would knock me off sooner or later. But he'd take me out clean, no body floating in Shit River—I'd be ground up and fed to some fat P.I. pigs, gone without a trace. I was up shit's creek, but I'd made my move and now it was checkmate time.

"KC, I need to hold your ride for a few days."

"Right on, Cap. Which one? The short or the scoot?"

"The short. What the fuck would I look like on

a damned scooter?"

"Black Captain America."

"Check it out, I need the Rover for a while. If I don't show after five days, it'll be at Maria's crib in Macati."

"Okay, Cap, you need some backup? I could run you up there. I'm on leave for another week."

Truth was, without Romeo I had no backup I could trust. But I didn't want a clean cat like KC getting into this shit.

"Streets, this deal is really heavy. I don't want to fuck up your career or get you bumped off on the humble because you're hanging with me."

"Look, Cappy, I'm a big boy. You want a driver, I'm your man. You say 'roll' and this boat's under way. Comprende?"

"Right on. Let's ruck up and roll."

KC grabbed his go bag, and we headed to Barrio Barretto and my hooch. I had my go bag ready and had another bag with my .38's, holsters, and ammunition. I told Nea I was going to finish this Goins thing for good, and that I loved her and would see her in a couple of days. She was tearing up as I kissed her good-bye. As KC and I pulled away, the lyric from *Hendrix's "Voodoo Child"* popped into my head. It went: *"If I don't see you no more in this world, I'll see you in the next one and don't be late, don't be late."* Man, it's weird the shit your mind can conjure up but I ain't no Voodoo Child, and I'd be back with Nea in a couple of days. This I felt in my heart.

The Rover was the perfect transport for the half-assed P.I. roads we traveled. We passed through many small farm villages and rice paddies, with lots of folks waving and smiling at the Yankees as we whizzed by. We stopped for food and some San Miguels along the way. As we approached the outskirts of the megacity, the concentration of people and buildings became dense. The mass poverty was still astounding to me, no matter how many times I saw it. A shantytown of millions. KC drops me off at Maria's apartment in Macati, a large luxury high-rise. Her brother, Carlos, lived there while she was on the road performing.

"KC, you go by Rolfie's at around 1530 tomorrow. He'll give you some instructions for me. You can call me here at this number."

I write down Maria's exchange and hand it to him.

"Okay, Cappy, I hope you know what time it is on this one. That cat Goins is ashes-to-ashes. No need for you to join him."

"KC, man, everything is everything."

We shake hands and KC reaches under his seat and pulls out a pewter half-pint flask.

"This is Pinch, not that syrup you drink. Say a toast with a sailor." He takes a long pull on the flask and says, "A rich man's home is his mansion." He passes the flask to me.

I take a hearty pull and say, "A sailor's home is the sea."

We each hit it again and say in unison, "A whiskey glass and a hooker's ass is home sweet home to me."

We shake hands again, and I say, "KC, man, I appreciate everything."

"Cap, it ain't no thing."

I walk into the building as KC pulls out into the crowded Macati traffic. They know me here, so the deskman greets me by name and informs me that neither Maria nor Carlos is in. I let him know I'll only be there for a day or two, and I use my key to let myself in. Maria's crib is immaculate, and her sound system is boss. I put some *Jobim* on and pour myself a Jack from the half gallon Maria keeps on hand in case I drop in.

In twenty-four hours from now, the rubber's going to hit the road. It'll be October 16, and Goins' death has been like a giant knot in my stomach these past nine and a half months. Maybe tomorrow I can untie it. I sipped at my Jack and got comfortable in Maria's pad. It could have been in New York, LA, or Tokyo: modern Scandinavian furniture, fake Rothkos, various plants, and a wall-sized aquarium filled with some mind-blowing exotic fish. After *Jobim*, I looked through her collection for something with brass. She, of course, had all the singers: *Ella, Sarah, Dinah, Billie, Betty, Joe Williams, Johnny Hartman*, and everything *Carmen McRae* ever recorded. I found some *Brownie, Morgan, and Miles*. I put *"Miles in the Sky"* on and poured another hook. I felt very calm, which was weird because I was putting myself into play on a game board that my suspect controlled, and I had no backup. I knew this could well be my last day on this side of the dirt. I thought about my go bag and my

.38s. Maybe when the shit started to stink, I could blast this motherfucker before I got knocked off.

At about 2330, KC called in to check the line. I'd had some second thoughts about staging at Maria's and told him I'd be at the Surfside Bar on Mabini Street. Before he hung up, he said, "Cap, I ain't going to let you walk into this shitstorm by your lonesome."

"Okay, Vato, we can hash that out tomorrow."

"All right, Ricky, but I ain't letting you take this sky dive alone.

"Later on, KC," I say, and hang up.

Maria had a Japanese-style hot tub, which I filled with water. As I sat, immersed over my shoulders, any tension that the Jack hadn't removed flowed from my mind and body into the hot water. I knew in my gut that within a few hours I'd be face-to-face with Goins' killer. I slept like a baby that night and got up at 0630 the next day. I did some calisthenics, followed by my three-S routine, then made a cup of instant Joe. I took a quick wash-up, got my gear together and went over my detective specials one more time. They were almost new. I got them straight from the factory and had the grips made to my specs. I was the only owner and user of these weapons. I straightened up the place and left Maria and Carlos a note letting them know I'd crashed there. I got a taxi to Mabini Street and was greeted by Johnny Bevins, the Surfside's Australian owner.

"Rick Baptiste, it's been a long time, mate."

"Too long, Johnny."

"You got that right, Rick."

"Look, Johnny, I need a flop. I'll be out by 2100."

"What's mine is yours, mate. You know where the private rooms are. Take number three," he says, throwing me the key.

I met Johnny in Da Nang in 1969, and he was one crazy-ass Aussie, but he ran this joint like a Playboy Club. No BS and no riff-raff, no dope, and no kids. Just prime A, number one Manila hookers. All business was cash on the barrelhead. The room is like a large single motel room with a king bed, nineteen-inch color TV, phone, and a bathroom with a shower. Johnny kept these rooms for his high-roller Japanese clients who he served some of the most beautiful college-girl hookers in Manila, all for top dollar. I called down to

Johnny, let him know KC was going to come calling in a few hours, and to send him up. As I'm laying my Roscoes' out on the bed to check them one more time. I put my rig on, made a couple of final adjustments, and practiced my simultaneous draw while I waited for KC with the invite to the party. Around 1700, there was a knock at the door, I opened it and KC walked in and handed me a small envelope. "Well, Cappy, here's your death warrant. Hope you're good with God," he says.

I made my up mind on this one a long time back, so everything is everything. If my number's up tonight, then it's my time to check out."

"All right, Sergeant Rock, open up them marching orders."

Which is what I proceeded to do. The directions were very clear and simple: "Be in front of the building where the pictures were taken at 2400 tonight, 10/17/76."

"Well, looks like midnight tonight is my date with destiny. He wants to meet at the spot the picture was taken. Problem is, I didn't shoot those flicks. What do you want me to do now?" KC asks.

"Here's a couple yards. Go back to Rolfie's and have him dig up that photog, ricky ticky," I say, handing KC two C-notes."

"Damn, Cap, what the fuck? You the godfather now?"

"I need this shit done quick, fast, and in a hurry—and money talks. Give those C's to Rolfie and tell him what I need, and he'll get it done."

"All right, Cap, I'll get back to you by eight."

"The sooner the better."

After KC leaves, I look my instructions over more closely. Once again, it's inside a small green envelope and card with no postmarks or identifying features. Even if I could run it for prints, I'm sure we would only find the delivery boy's, Rolfie's, and KC's. This cat I'm dealing with is a double-dealing, opportunistic, sociopath—not much different from a lot of ambitious, greedy MF's. What I'm counting on is that his arrogance and sense of superiority over someone like me will make him show his ass. The fact that I peeped the big picture makes me a threat to him, and breathing fresh air above ground a luxury for me.

At 1930, KC called to tell me that Rolfie had

run down the photog, who was also the taxi driver and pimp. It was set up so that at 2100 hours he would carry me to the spot where the picture was shot. It cost a yard, the most expensive cab ride in Manila.

At 2034 there's a tap on the door, followed by KC's voice. "Open up, Cap." I open the door and a stern-looking KC walks in and sits on the bed. "Cap, you ain't riding this out with me on the bench. I got my rig in the Rover, and I know the spot you're going to—Sangley Point. Hell, I was stationed there before I met you."

"Look KC, this ain't just a 'dope-boy bump-off.' It's high-echelon government spy-versus-spy shit. You just being around me could get your cornflakes pissed on for life. You're putting your ass on a heavy line."

"Yeah, Cap, it's my ass, and it's been on lots of lines—most of which I didn't choose. I'm choosing this one. I'm going out there, finding some high ground, and giving you some cover. There ain't shit else you can tell me, Cap."

I knew there was no changing his military mind. KC had been a PBR[24] boy in Nam and could handle any weapon from a rocket

---

[24] PBR – Patrol Boat Riverine

propelled grenade to a BB gun. He manned the .50 calibers on these boats and had a Navy Cross and a few Purple Hearts. Bravery was not the question. But maybe, as with me, his sanity was.

"Okay KC, still all for one."

"You got that right, Cap."

We shake hands and exchange bear hugs. As KC leaves, I realize I was trying to get Romeo, who's already dirty, to back me up. But I guess the man upstairs figured me and KC would take this tour together.

At 2100 hours, there's another rap on my door. I open it and a tall, slim Filipino walks in and introduces himself as Felemon Bastemante. He has gray flecks in his hair and mustache, sharp eyes and facial features—a mestizo.

"So, you were the tail on my guy. Photog, taxi driver and pimp, that was outstanding work."

"Not so hard. I have many operatives and to the whites, we all look alike."

"I heard that. How long will it take to get to the location?"

"It'll take maybe one hour. I drive you to Sangley Point, take you to the building, and that's all. After I drop you, I'm out. You get back on your own."

It's 2115 when we leave the Surfside, which has a few customers, and girls engaging in commerce. The taxi ride through the nighttime Manila streets is still loud and colorful, but less chaotic than during the daylight hours. We head to the port of Manila, where Sangley Point was once a port and dry dock for the US 7th Fleet, until a few years ago when it was turned back over to the Philippine government. Felemon was a closed-mouthed dude, not saying squat until we got out to an abandoned part of the old base.

"That building there, number 182, is where I take pictures. The white man met several times with three Chinese. Same three people each time. Two men and a tall woman."

"You think the others were Chinese?"

"No think. I hear them talk after the white man would leave."

That verified my scenario. True to his word, Felemon left me on my own near building 182, an old warehouse with scant illumination from lights mounted on the building itself, and a streetlight about fifty yards away. It was 2225,

308

and I knew that I would be face-to-face with agent double cross soon, he would have to stifle my ass with lead or money.

There were a few barrels and dumpsters on the concrete surrounding the warehouse. The only high ground was another warehouse about a quarter mile away, and way in the distance, maybe a half mile or more, was an old crane. I took residence between a dumpster and the warehouse. It was a waiting game now, and time seemed to move in slow motion. The air was close and thick, and the only sounds I could hear, other than the water lapping at the piers, were the port rats scurrying around. In the distance you could vaguely hear the mechanical sound of cranes loading and unloading container ships.

At 2400 exactly, a Mercedes sports coupe rolls up, stops, cuts the lights and the motor. The muscular, pony-tailed figure I had counted on seeing steps out smoking a Panatela cigar, carrying an attaché case.

"Baptiste, you can come out. Let's get this game over."

"All right, Franco. Or is it Zimmerman? Show-and-tell time," I say as I emerge from my blind, walking toward him.

"What's in a name, my friend? I've had many in my lifetime. Like the hippies used to say, 'Brand names are immaterial.' Call me what you will."

"Well, how does 'murderer and traitor' grab your ass? Let's just cut to the chase. I want Goins' name cleared and his family taken care of."

"Look, my man, you're way out of your pay grade. This is about national security, not some spade who got greedy. Goins was collateral damage."

"I peeped your slimy ass. I know you smuggled that prowler aircraft through the Jungle to trade to the Chi-Com for cash and China white. The same communist we've been fighting since Korea. That's treason, in my book."

"Well, Baptiste, your book doesn't have all the pages. That aircraft was a gift, a good-faith gesture from Uncle Sam to the PRC. Our two countries have a common enemy, the Soviets, and the enemy of our enemy, is our friend. China's going to become our ally, and partner, that's realpolitik, way above your piss-ant pay grade."

I had taken my glasses off and could see the arrogant smirk on his face. I could count the hairs in his eyebrows, as all my senses came into super sharpness. His breath sounded like the wind as he calmly blew smoke from his cigar.

"That realpolitik may be above my pay grade but putting Goins on ice and dealing that China white with those communists is right up my alley. Goins was going to dime your sorry ass, so you offed him. You fucked up, though, leaving his body around. You ain't worth a good goddamn."

"What I'm worth depends on the client. Now, you on the other hand, Baptiste, are worth much less than a good goddamn, but there's fifty thousand US cash in this briefcase," he says as he opens the case and shows me a neat brick of yard notes. "You can take it and walk away. It's a prime deal."

"How about 'Fuck you, you prime motherfucker?' I've seen how your 'prime deals' work out."

At that, Franco looks at me, smirking. He raises his cigar and says, "Your call, my man. But when this smoke hits the deck, you can kiss your ass good-bye."

"See you in hell," I say, reaching for my roscoes' as Franco releases the cigar, which I watch tumble to the ground, seemingly in slow motion. My Colts clear leather just as the cigar hits the ground and Franco topples over. My guns are in my hand, unfired. I scramble for cover, hoping it was KC who made that shot, but figuring if it wasn't him, whoever popped Franco wouldn't leave any loose ends.

After what seemed like an hour of no human sound or movement, I hear a vehicle approach. Looking out from my hideaway, I can see the lights of a Land Rover coming toward my location. The Rover stops near Franco's body. The lights and motor are cut off, and KC gets out and takes cover behind the vehicle. I give a whistle, to which KC responds in kind. As I emerge from my cut, KC walks around the Rover, M-14 in hand. We both stop at Franco's body.

"Streets, that was a hell of a shot. Where was your blind?"

"Man, that wasn't my shot. I was on that warehouse, I didn't have a clean shot. That shot had to come from off that crane over there," KC says, pointing to the tall structure off in the distance.

"What the fuck? That's damn near a half mile out at zero dark thirty. Who the hell could have made that shot?" As I say this, I already know. I roll Franco over, and the gaping hole where his left eye used to be, told me the name of that tune.

I was summoned to the US Embassy in Manila to meet with Morris. He debriefed me on certain aspects of the Goins/Franco case. He repeated much of what Franco had laid out—realpolitik, and so on. They'd been watching Franco for some time. This wasn't his first rogue act. What I gleaned from Morris was that it was neither the Goins murder nor drug-running that did Franco in. It was his sloppiness on such a big operation that made him a liability and, therefore, expendable. Morris praised my skills as an agent and again asked me to join his outfit. Again, I declined. He also let me know that the bullet that took Franco out could just as easily have popped my dome. I couldn't shake the feeling that I'd been used as bait and as a fall guy right from Jump Street.

Goins name was cleared, and his family received his survivor pay. No mention was made of Franco's briefcase, so KC and I split the fifty large right down the middle. I kept five grand and sent the rest to Goins' mother for his kids.

KC got his promotion to senior chief photographer's mate at the Fleet Reserve Club in early December. The party that ensued after his promotion was buck wild, with the twins from Daktari dancing nude on the bar, and all the guests juiced to the max. He moved the twins in with him, Mimi and Fifi. Old KC was fast becoming the sultan of Subic Bay.

POSTSCRIPT

I'm sitting in the cool confines of Papa Joe's Green Dolphin drinking Jack on ice, dragging on a Kool, and digging *Grant Green's* version of the Beatles' *"A Day in the Life."* The image of the dead young girl in those shoes with those dolls haunts me. While I was busy crackin' the Goins case, Denny B continued the investigation into her murder. He mentioned something about a tall, bald VP flyboy named Schultz who was rotated to CONUS on the ricky ticky back in September, around the time we discovered the girl's body. I was mulling over that bit of intel when Romeo walked up to the bar and ordered a Bombay tonic.

"Capone, looks like you in the big leagues now."

"Yeah, tell me about it."

"Ain't nothing to tell, Homes. That deal with Franco and Morris - Uncle Sam and Chairman Mao, it's all just business. Cash money, baby. Ain't no good guys here; the CIA, the Government, Goins, everyone's dirty. Those fools just hide behind their titles and three-piece suits, ya dig?" Romeo said.

"I can dig it, Bro. The U.S. Government plays all sides of the street, some guys are Ivy League

315

suits like Morris, while others are stone gangsters like the Frogs. The Government was behind Goins murder, the Frogs, and the whole scheme of the technology transfer." Romeo was right, it's all about the money.

Romeo turns up his Bombay, daps me a short time, turns to split, then looks back and says, "Speaking of the Frogs, they send their love." He walks out laughing his crazy-assed high-pitched giggle.

"What the hell was that loony mother-jumper yapping about?" Joe asks.

"Pop's keep pouring that Jack. I got one hell of a P.I. tale to tell you."

Made in the USA
Middletown, DE
11 March 2022

62283444R00191